"I walked that 850 miles into Indian Territory with the Feathers family and never regretted a moment. The author's ability to tell a story makes readers want to buy a black light and make a night raid on the Cimarron. Read the mix of family history, Native American folklore, and military realism. You will not be able to put this book down."

CW4 L. Feather (Ret)

"Taste the dust on the trail; feel the heartache of being forced to leave their homes, struggle toward the land set aside called Indian Territory. Hardships, exhilaration, fear, death at every turn, yes these were the people that helped build the great state of Oklahoma. Pat has written a touching story about the ancients that made the journey from the southern tier of states into the wild land. His own ancestors traveled the Trail of Tears, wrote the hide pictographs, told the stories in their own language, gave of them selves in *Lone*. A uniquely American story of love."

L. Rothgeb
Cousin Jack Lorett

"Remarkable to watch Pat transcend generations with such insight and detail. For many years we have delighted in his story-telling talents. The writer will transport you back in time to see, feel, and experience the lessons of life as our ancestors learned them."

Ray & Jean Demuth

LONE

LONE

A NOVEL BY PAT LORETT

5-7-09

To Ray & Jean,

Thank you for reading
for us. We hope you enjoy
reading this book.

Pat & Shorty

TATE PUBLISHING & *Enterprises*

Published by Tate Publishing & Enterprises, LLC
127 E. Trade Center Terrace | Mustang, Oklahoma 73064 USA
1.888.361.9473 | www.tatepublishing.com

Tate Publishing is committed to excellence in the publishing industry. The company reflects the philosophy established by the founders, based on Psalm 68:11,
"The Lord gave the word and great was the company of those who published it."

Book design copyright © 2009 by Tate Publishing, LLC. All rights reserved.
Cover design by Janae J. Glass
Interior design by Lindsay B. Behrens

Published in the United States of America

ISBN: 978-1-60799-313-1
1. Fiction / Historical   2. Fiction / Sagas
09.03.20

Lives were needlessly spent on the Trail of Tears, most left to rot without a grave. Land ravaged by humans that were so hungry they ate everything raw. The Miner clan braved the trail west, finding nothing that resembled home, knowing they could never go back, not wanting to go forward. Children fed on whatever they could catch. Salvation was found in the form of a little ole man that fed the masses by trading his beans and corn for whatever a person could trade.

Miner Feather ushered the native tribes into the modern age. And now his secrets are about to be revealed.

The Black Hawk slipped almost silently onto the sandbar of the Cimarron River. A panel light mirrored the taut face of Chief Feather, while the magnetic range finder located the bridge that spanned the river. A quick side scan lost the bridge in the fog, and his mind wondered if the Indian spirits were pulling tricks on him again. It seemed an age since his father, Lone, had run these same riverbanks. The night had been spent hunting for the bridge, his locater had lied to him, and here he was on the sandbar, looking through the most modern equipment of the age, lost again.

TABLE OF CONTENTS

SERVICE

The Black Hawk slipped almost silently onto the sandbar of the Cimarron River. The only light on the instru-
ment panel mirrored the taunt face of Chief Feather,
while his magnetic range finder located the bridge that
spanned the Cimarron River of old. A quick side scan
lost the bridge in the river fog, and his mind wondered
if the Indian sprits were pulling tricks on him again.
It seemed an age since his father, Lone, had run these
same river banks with his buddy, Pat. The night had
been spent hunting for the bridge. His locater had
lied to him. *Maybe they can make some sense of those old
records.*

The concrete abutments were still up on the hill;
the river had washed the bridge downstream and had a
party piling all that sand on it. I quickly dipped myself
in the river again and slogged my wet boots into the
modern cell called a cockpit. My flight clothes didn't
like my wet, sandy body and resisted going back on. I

turned the electronics back on and made a slide scan copy of the horizontal plain called the Cimarron River. As my rotor was coming up to speed, Fox One was complaining that I had a twenty-million-dollar aircraft set down in the river bottom and wanted a complete explanation. I opened the side window and let the slip-stream drown out my report.

"Fox One, the fog is so thick you have to cut it with a lance."

"Lone One you are going to have to climb out of the river before I can understand you." That satisfied the sergeant. When my locater had lied to him, and here he was down on the river sandbar, looking through the most modern equipment of the age, lost again.

The radio crackled him back into the modern time and demanded to know why he was sitting in the center of the Cimarron River.

"Fox One, this is Lone One, those coordinates you gave me for the Radiker Bridge are off about one thousand meters. Either that or the river has moved the bridge to another location. I'll be back in the air as soon as I can see through the fog."

"Lone One, you have fog penetrating capabilities on your aircraft. I assume you have been trained to use the modern equipment?"

"Fox One, you are cutting out. I will pick you up when I get air born."

I'll let that sergeant stew on his own airway awhile, and maybe I can figure out what happened to the bridge.

The twin turbine engines unwound to a soft purr and let me hear the ways of the water. I had run around on this same river sandbar when I was a kid not four years old. Those river smells came back in a rush as I stepped from the modern age to my own ancient past. I left my helmet and clothes in that modern war machine and was one with the river. I couldn't resist a quick dip in the red, warm water and found the bridge steel buried under a million tons of sand. *Well, well, the past is present; wait till I tell this to the map department.* My rotor speed was up, I lifted the Black Hawk and did a vertical scan for a mile on each side of the abutments. I pushed save, and my mission was filed for download when I arrived back at Fort Sill, Oklahoma.

I sat down on my pad some sixty air minutes later, unloaded my report to a hard copy, and told the air jockey to clean the sand out of my Black Hawk. I right quick took a shower and hid my flight suit in my locker, washed all that red dirt out of my boots, stashed them in an unused locker, and was ready for my report at General Lance's demand for my attendance in the flight office. I right-smart saluted my commanding officer and laid the report on his desk.

"Chief Feather, what in the slipstream were you doing on a sandbar of the Cimarron River?"

"Sir, the night's instructions were to find the Radiker Bridge take a scan, and bring the results. I found the bridge one thousand meters downstream of the abutments, buried under the sand bottom. The air sergeant got all bent out of shape that he couldn't reach me when I sat down on a sandbar to check out the location of the bridge."

"*Stop!* Chief Feather, we have the most advanced piece of aircraft in the world, and you are telling me that the air sergeant couldn't reach you three hundred miles from your pad at night?"

"Sir, you should have a recording of my transmission at the air marshals' tower."

"Chief Feather, be seated and I will have that recording post haste."

I hope that sergeant had his tapes going tonight. I heard, no, I felt the message come over the computer and was relieved when indeed the message was garbled with air static. My commanding officer didn't let me off until he had checked my scanning of the river bottoms.

"Chief Feather, everything seems in order. The only point that I want to make at this time is that you left your twenty-million-dollar aircraft with all the modern secrets of the age sitting on an unstable sandbar, completely unmanned for a period of at least an hour. We can't even imagine the aboriginal intent of the local population. You are dismissed."

I just then received a written note to see my air jockey about my craft. My brown buddy, the air jockey; yes, he was as brown as me and from another tribe. Indeed, he had cleaned the red sand out of my cabin and was set to have a good grin as I came back. His salute went unanswered as I could see he was up to something.

"Sergeant, you left me a note to see you," I said.

"Yes, sir," he spoke smartly.

"Sergeant, just tell me what you have up your sleeve."

A knowing grin got my attention as he pulled a spirit circle out of his vest to show me. "Chief Feather, you should be careful who you meet down on the Cimarron River bottoms. This spirit circle was tied on your aircraft with its eagle feathers intact; there is no telling what these Indians intend to do about us landing on their land! Oh, and sir, you saved something on your computer; I couldn't get into the folder because of your password. You might want to take that off."

I thanked my air jockey and punched in my password. As the scans came off, I wondered why I had saved them, but here they were in my hot hands. The delete button erased my input, and I opened the mainframe and deleted the whole night's conversations. I thanked my air jockey and knew the spirit circle was safe in his possession.

WHAT THE ANCIENT KNEW

The wagon compartment was almost full of gold-lead ingots. My lead mine had taken a dark turn in history as the last pages of the Indians' disposition unraveled. All the commerce of the tribe had been seized by the United States government; any show of insurrection put you on the nearest trail going west. Atlanta, Georgia, became the hub leading you to the red rock country out west that most people called Indian Territory.

My family had been mining the lead mine for several decades, making lead balls for rifles of the age. The problem with our lead mine was that it had begun producing very fine gold of copious quantities. It was problematic for an Indian to have a lavish lifestyle amongst the starving clans. This colored metal was a problem for an Indian to dispose of. I poured and sized balls of gold, then dipped them in lead where they looked like lead shot. The mystery of hiding all that gold was solved with a long, double-bottomed wagon. It took me two years to completely fill the bottom of our Conestoga wagon with enough gold to last the rest of our life. I never told anybody of my scheme to sustain our remnant.

My Feather clan started the trail ride in 1810 from Walnut Grove, Georgia, to start anew in the land called Indian Territory. We had eighteen in our wagon train and several herds of horses, cows, and domestic stock. The Feather clan had been buying up old wagons, mismatched teams, red-spotted cattle, and taking all the dogs we could get to follow our wagon train. We had decided to not take baths while on the trail, wearing breechcloths and buckskins, anything to melt into the local tribes moving west.

We left one night, much to the delight of the militia, anything to get rid of that mess of brown skins. We had a doctor, guides, and a linguist that could speak several languages, two collage graduates from Harvard, guards aplenty that could shoot the eye out of a squirrel, cooks and wagon supplies. Our outriders were scantly-clad, full-fledged braves armed with bows and arrows; each wagon had Kentucky rifles ready to load if the need arose. Our guide had all the maps of the time and knew the exact course we would take to Indian Territory. The United States had bought the Louisiana Purchase in 1803, and we had a map of the territory that showed the main rivers. I melted back into the background being my own self, a lead miner on the trail.

My final act in Walnut Grove was to dynamite my lead mine so nobody would ever see what I had taken from the bowels of the earth. As far as I could tell, all the gold had been taken out and most of the lead was covered with twenty feet of rock. I dusted my hands off and left that old way of life for the ancients to haunt.

CALL UP

"Chief Feather, report to the map department" came over the system. I rat-tailed through the confines of the base and reported to a new recruit.

The receptionist read my faded nametag. "Chief Feather, you are expected down the hall in the map department."

I slouched in and sat down in a soft divan that about swallowed my whole body. The orderly of the day came and invited me to the map of central Oklahoma. "*Well, well, this is going to be good*", I thought. All of my reports from the night before were spread-eagled on the lighted tables. A map jockey introduced himself to me as Master Sergeant Dick Tells and explained the Standard Operating Procedure (SOP) of identifying the Cimarron River, namely where the Radiker Bridge was supposed to be.

"Chief Feather, we have a discrepancy that we are trying to decipher and wanted to talk to you about what you saw last night on the river."

I waited for a stagnant pause and said, "Nothing."

You could have heard a pin drop, and then the whole department exploded into hilarious laughter. This was swallowed in a gulp as the commanding officer straightened up and demanded to know why I hadn't seen the spook standing beside my Black Hawk Helicopter.

"Why I, ah, ah, don't know what you are talking about, General Lance."

"Chief Feather, I want you to look at the night scope video taken out the side of your aircraft while you were off playing in the Cimarron River."

I wondered if there were tapes that might ground me for the rest of my life. The orderly reran my night scope. Out of the fog, an apparition drifted up to the side and looked in to the nose of the camera. This thirty-second snippet ran several times, and I had them stop at full-face exposure. Take the war paint off of the face, and here was a man about my height who looked way too much like me. General Lance spoke, and I quote: "Chief, we need to talk privately!"

A quick-called briefing of more brass put me in the hot seat. I told everything that I had done last night; my shoes and flight suit were produced as evidence. I told them my twin brother, Sam, was a trickster, and how he knew I was going to be on that sandbar in the middle of the night was a mystery. I surmised that he was just out prowling around the area and happened to be there. We returned to the map department, and it was decided to take a recon of the area in the daylight, take plenty of pictures, and report back for another tabletop discussion. We scheduled flight, and I noticed we had plenty of witnesses.

Flight time was 0400 the next morning, and that put us on that sandbar before daylight. I did a thermal scan of the horizon for the unfriendly, drew a blank and stood by at the controls just in case of trouble. The aircraft settled down crazy. I thought, *"it's those spooks again."*

The camera crew jumped out, promptly sunk up to their belt line, and set up a howl: "It's a trap!" I felt the ship yaw sideways and the landing gear sunk in the quicksand. I applied full power to the rotor, and there we sat, a twenty million-dollar Black Hawk up to its belly in the most ancient of river traps! Part of the landing gear snapped, and the other one bent out of shape before we sprang thirty feet in the air. I leveled out and could just see the camera crew squealing like a bunch of pigs in a wallow. I let back down, and the crew was able to drop enough lines to save the camera crew from a wet, sandy, drowning death. They no more than got back into the ship, and my thermal scanner started sounding off. We had unfriendly company.

I heard the first arrow strike my bubble windshield. *If that had been a fifty caliber, I would be dead now,* I pulled back from the line of fire. As the door slid shut, an arrow with a stone point stuck in the thigh of a camera crewman. I thought at that moment, *the debriefing will take the rest of the day.* A big handful of sterile gauze staunched the flow of blood, and we headed for base with the wounded.

Fox One came on the air and wanted to know if we had found the old bridge. I informed General Lance that we had wounded and to clear the helipad on the base hospital; we would land in sixty minutes. *When this day started, I just knew that something was going to happen on that old Indian land, but never this.* I flew in sight of the flight tower and promptly received a command to not land on the helipad but to report to maintenance on the flight line. I reported again that we had wounded aboard and that I needed to land on the hospital helipad.

"Negative, Lone One, you have an obstruction hanging from your craft. Hover over the maintenance truck until they can clear this off."

If this day ever ends, it will be a miracle, I thought to myself.

My air jockey was standing on top of his service truck with an air ratchet and dropped the broken wheel on the tarmac. He gave the launch signal, and I hovered the Black Hawk on the helipad to off load my wounded crew. They scrambled away from the craft like I was a spook. The air jockey had new gear, and we reversed the action over the service truck till I was whole again. My trip to my landing pad was completely filled with commands from General Lance. I immediately downloaded audio, video, scan results of the riverbanks before and after the attack and locked my computer with my password.

More brass, General Lance, and the complete map department was standing, ready to string me to that twenty-million-dollar airship in the conference room when I cleared the base command doors. General Lance took command of the situation and called for the flight plan of the day. I had my papers all in order and started melting them into his hand. Each report was given a thorough scan, copied, and passed around. The side scan radar was displayed on the overhead screen and reran several times to satisfy the persecutors;

video of my reaction to the emergency was examined with that same scrutiny; cockpit voiceover came at the exact second of the actions. The first arrow was aimed at my head, and I jumped sideways when the video and sound captured the moment it struck my bubble. The hail of arrows bounced off my precious capsule, and one stuck in the thigh of a crewman. The rest of the video was flight time, emergency repairs, offloading of the wounded, the repair of the skids, and the touch down on my pad.

General Lance accepted all the reports and dismissed the map department to their task. "Gentlemen I believe we have a complete folder of reports from Chief Feather. I'm going to dismiss this meeting at the present time, and if there are further reports, we will stay in touch. Chief Feather stay with me for a continued meeting. I expect a report from the map department, and we want to go over this with you."

"Yes, sir. In fact, could I go change my flight suit and freshen up, maybe get some chow?"

"Negative, Chief Feather, you are under base arrest for destroying United States government property. The military police escorts will accompany your every action until further notice."

And I thought I was going to have an easy day! My trip to the shower drew the scuttlebutt news from the cracks of Fort Sill. I took my old sweet time and contemplated the spirit circle given to my aircraft. My air jockey and I were the only men that knew about those eagle feathers. *I believe I will leave the spirits in the Black Hawk!*

The map department brought the results of the morning, and I was dismissed with my attendant base guards in tow.

TRAIL OF TEARS

From a spectator's viewpoint, our Feathers clan was the usual rag-tag group traveling to Indian Territory. The elders warned us to not to speak the English that we had been taught in school. The only languages we used were Cherokee and universal signing. We again swore everybody to secrecy and to never talk with the militia about anything. All the squaws wore the traditional dress and hid the children in their skirts. The men wore breechcloths with blankets for the night chills. It must have worked because we seldom were watched or checked out.

Fare was game off the land that we could kill or dig with a pointed stick. We took on the way of life of our ancestors and hid our true identity. My team was a mismatched pair of draft horses, then a black-and-brown pair of mules in front. Every day before we got on the trail, we smeared mud on our faces to hide behind, and I had to paint a down-turned smile to hide my true self.

I never told my clan about the gold covered with lead shot that I was carrying and soon was able to get on with the life that was being dealt out to us.

My first major river was almost my last. As the high-wheeled Conestoga wagon plied the deep waters of the Tennessee River, it sank like a floundered boat. My teams were swimming all they could, and the only thing that saved the wagon were the ropes that were tied to it. We took a second look at my wagon, and animal fat was spread over the outside. I was ready for the next major waterway. The families complained of the rancid fat smell until the young braves threw dirt on the fat, and that hid my secret for the complete trip.

Nights on the trail were fraught with danger as there were way too many questionable people on the trail, all of them hungry. Our outriders had a full-time job guarding our troupe, and the dogs that followed along soon paid for their keep. We had left Walnut Grove, Georgia, in the wintertime; we had good days, but cold nights to travel.

Our best watchdog turned out to be a young donkey of mine that just kind of followed us along; I can't remember if she ever wore a halter. The kids would pile on her in the daytime to catch a free ride. We tried to bunch the wagons up at night and hide from the night sounds. When the donkey started sleeping in the wagon circle, we never knew, or maybe she taught us where to stop. The elders smiled and put all the praise on old Long Ears. She had a heehaw that could wake the dead, and sure enough, she woke the circle of dogs. They got to barking and we had a full-fledged raid going about us by the time we got awake. We thought the raid was a traveling tribe from the way they were screeching. The Kentucky rifles came out of hiding and spoke a cannon shot that was the rally cry of our troupe. Several bow shots brought down their share of the enemy, and complete silence took over the campsite. A fire was rekindled, and firebrands counted six white outlaws shot from the saddles.

The first reaction was to run, the second was to call the militia, and the third was to drag all the evidence into the woods and give them a Christian burial. We didn't know what to do, but dragging those white men to their graves put the whole troupe to work in the middle of the night. The horses were stripped of their saddles and all tack was buried with the men. We turned the horses in with our stock and they soon ran with our ponies. All signs of bloodshed were brushed out with branches, and we left this site with heavy hearts. I just knew the deed would be found out, and we would be hung from the trees without ever telling our side.

Daylight found us on the trail. We saw the militia, acted dumb, tried to sign, and they left this stinkin' tribe to movin' on. We stumbled out of their sight and made time looking sick as long Ears had the last say with her long, drawn out heehaw. We didn't know what to call our guard donkey until one of the youngest came up with L'ear, and the name stuck. We traveled as long as there was light and then some; our need was to hide in the background.

Our travels took us to the next waterway. We felt, no, heard the Mississippi long before we looked across the great expanse of water. We had been on the trail and were so tired that we decided to take time to refresh our selves. This turned out to be the best choice as we got to see the river travels. We caught fish the size of our dogs, shot geese with our bows and arrows, and found out how to cross the river.

The militia came one day with an interpreter and signed a question asking if we were going to Indian Territory. One of the old elders signed that yes, we had to cross the river and didn't know how. We didn't tell him that we had seen a paddleboat barge pick up throngs of Indians and take them to the other side. We must have looked so dumb and helpless; the signer told of a barge that would take our whole clan over to the other side if we had horses for trade. Our elder sat straight-faced and signed that we had two that we could let them have. A deal was struck for the portage; we rounded up two of the raiding party horses and made the trade as the barge was loaded with our clan. We took as many extra Indians as they would let us and chugged across the muddy Mississippi that day. Without a doubt, that was the easiest trip we made on the way to Indian Territory.

Our hearts were broken that day seeing all the fellow Indians being forced to walk all the way to the land promised by the United States government. Our pressing need was trying to act dumb and not draw attention to our clan. I hoped that we looked in need as much as the next man. We came into Arkansas and found a settlement called Little Rock, which we avoided. There was no need to have any contact with the outside world until we approached Indian Territory.

Spirit Mission

I took my own sweet time showering, changing into fatigues, and had another call to General Lance's office. My guides made it look like I was under arrest, much to their delight. I was escorted into his inner office, and my guards were dismissed for the time being. *Foot, I was enjoying their company!*

General Lance and I were meeting with base inquiries, and I knew right then I was entangled with trouble. "Chief Feather this is Mr. Ables with a formal complaint from the Cherokee Indian Tribe of Oklahoma stating that you knowingly sat a Black Hawk helicopter down on Indian land on the night of 4 August 2008. This complaint wants to know why you sat this helicopter down in Indian land. To refresh your mind, Chief Feather, this is the night you were sent to the Radiker Bridge by the map department to scan the discrepancy of a missing bridge. Do you understand, Chief?"

"Yes, sir. General Lance, in my report of 4 August 2008, the bridge was indeed missing, and since I knew there had been a large flood on the Cimarron River, I suspected the main bridge had been washed down river. I sat my Black Hawk in the center of the sandbar, waded out to the burial site, and found the bridge spans in approximately twenty feet of water and sand. In my report, I radioed Fox One that I had found the bridge, took side scans of the wreck, and reported back to the base. I filed all my reports with the map department, and they are in their files at this time."

Mr. Ables asked General Lance why he was calling me Chief Feather. "In all of my papers of the Cherokee Nation, I do not have any Chief Feather."

General Lance looked the civilian over and explained that Mr. Lone Feather was in deed Chief Warrant Officer Fourth Class of the United States Army, and he would be addressed Chief Feather.

Mr. Ables asked me if I had taken anything from the river or left anything on the sandbar. "Yes sir, Mr. Ables, my helicopter took a face picture of my brother, Sam, standing beside my helicopter, looking into the camera lens. I left my footprints in the sand, and I took the sand that was on my boots. My air jockey can verify the sand; he washed that sand out of my cabin and down the pad drain where my aircraft is tied down."

General Lance asked if Mr. Ables had any more questions. "General Lance, I don't have any more questions at this time, but I suggest that Chief Feather be confined to the base until this matter is cleared up."

"Yes, Chief Feather is under base arrest at this time. Okay, Mr. Ables, you might as well know about the next day," General Lance injected.

"Stop, General Lance, this is the complete text of the complaint. If you have other information, that will have to be dealt with later."

I'm glad that we're not at war with the Cherokee Nation. There will never be a war fought, only words!

Mr. Ables took his leave as General Lance motioned for me to have a seat. He wasn't finished.

"Chief Feather, would you like a cup of coffee? All this military jargon has made me thirsty." *Ah, I surmise we will get something done now.* An attendant brought the coffee, and we sat down to business.

"Chief Feather, I like your thoroughness. We have jammed every type of question to you, and here are all your reports on my desk. Now, off the record, and I guarantee there are no recording devices in my office, what else can go wrong with you landing on a sandbar in the Cimarron River—besides going skinny dipping in the best warm water in the state, leaving your side window open while trying to talk to my Fox One. Please, tell me what is going to happen."

"General, will you call in clearance for me to fly you down to the Cimarron River? I want to show you something."

"Anything to get this cleared up. I need some flight time anyway."

General Lance made the necessary arrangements; we donned flight suits and met up inside my Black Hawk. *I hope this turns out well,* I thought. I sat on the tarmac and disabled every video, listening device, and cockpit recording device that was on my aircraft. The General looked on and shook his head like *what kind of a nut do I have here?* My air jockey gave me the thumbs up, and I lifted off. I set the flight at a leisurely pace, set down on a sandbar on the north side of the Cimarron, and tried to raise Fox One. Absolute silence.

"Okay, General Lance, we can talk now. The base cannot hear us, and there is no recording in this aircraft."

General Lance sighed. "Chief Feather, there is more to you than you are telling. Please fill me in."

It was my turn to sigh, and I started my story right before the Indian Territories were formed. "Sir, you know that I'm full-blood Cherokee Indian?"

"Yes, Chief Feather, I have read your service reports. There isn't much from your youth, but your service in Iraq and Kuwait has been noteworthy."

"Thank you, General Lance, but this is not why I have brought you to my place of birth. I was born on top of that bluff on the south side of the river; my old home place burned down a few years ago, and there is hardly a black spot left. The only thing left is a teepee of my brother's that he set up last year.

"It is by coincidence that you sent me on that fact-finding mission for the map department. I didn't pay to much attention to the coordinates until I stepped out of my Black Hawk the other night. It was like a turn back to my childhood, and I couldn't resist taking a skinny dip. I knew that the old river bridge had washed out, and I never paid too much attention to all those old tales of my family. I saw, no, I *felt* my brother come out of the fog and dance around my aircraft. I don't know, but I bet he tried to put a spell on all these electronics. He left me this," I said as I produced the spirit circle.

"This in itself is a good omen, but coming back the next day was an intrusion of the river spirits. The next day, we got into a quicksand pit that wasn't there the night before. I know that my brother has caused you some anxious feelings the last two days, but I ask you to bear with me, and I will get it cleared up."

General Lance took the spirit circle and started his examination. I felt the wind and told General Lance to hold on because we had to leave immediately. By the time I got those twin turbines producing power, my ship was rocking violently. I hove to and barely missed the limbs and sand trying to destroy us. General Lance had turned that certain white color that all men resort to when the unexplained has manifested. We flew back over ourselves and almost immediately, the aircraft settled back to normal flight. I took us out of sight of the river to sit back down in a field.

"Lone One, we saw you on the radar. Is your mission complete?"

"Fox One, this is General Lance. *No,* our mission is not complete, and I will contact you when we depart."

"Oookay, Fox One, we have a Mr. Ables on the horn that wants an appointment with you ASAP."

"Fox One, I will fill him in on the present situation when I return." General Lance turned to me and said, "Chief Feather, turn on all the instrumentation that this ship can muster. I want to see for myself a complete scan of the river in question."

"Now we get something done," I mumbled to myself. I cranked a complete set of dials until the Black Hawk could have glowed in the dark and flew up river until we were well past the abutments of the old river bridge called Radiker. Turning down river, we started our deep scanning of the south side, going east. As we got even with Yonder Rock, there sat my brother, cross-legged, watching the show. I made sure we got his smiling face and the complete sand-covered structure of the bridge.

Our return to base was one of quietness. The only words were, "Download two copies of everything, one for me and one for you."

As the copies finished, General Lance commanded that a complete delete of today's activities was carried out, even in the mainframe onboard computer. "Chief Feather, I'm censoring all your activities until this matter is cleared up. You are confined to the base without escort. No phone calls, except in my office in front of me, is that clear?"

"Yes, sir, General Lance."

SMALLPOX

Our flight away from Little Rock, Arkansas, couldn't have come at a better time. We started smelling rotting flesh, namely the dead Indians pulled out away from the trails. We could not believe that a nation would treat human beings so inhumanely. Our doctor warned us to not have any contact with anybody, just keep moving west. I can't remember the first person of our group to come down with the spotted skin, but I was last in the group of wagons. Whoever was sick rode downwind until either dead or cured. I was thankful my teams had learned to follow by this time, because fever racked my thin frame for days on end.

I awoke one morning three weeks later to complete silence. We were parked in a circle, and from the position of the sun, it was close to the noon meal. I could just see the stock all standing in the shade. L'ear was standing by my wagon, chewing her cud, the dogs were all asleep, and I supposed I was the only person that survived the smallpox. No, I could hear snoring, a baby crying. The camp was at a complete standstill. I took another nap and woke up again to complete silence. I heard someone walking about and tried to cry out; all I could do was whisper. That seemed to be enough, as the doctor came and stood by my wagon box, and I didn't recognize my good friend. He had a complete set of smallpox growing all over his hide. He asked me if I could sit up and take some soup and water. I whispered "yes," and he told me to come feed some of the others that were worse off. I thought, *how can anybody feel worse than me?*

I asked how many we had lost. The doctor said we had lost two squaws and one small brave. I did notice the large smallpox sign painted on each wagon. It must have been enough to keep the militia at bay and anybody else that had visions of robbing us. Another week passed before we were able to make tracks west. The stock was well rested, we were able to bury our dead, and the doctor left the signs on the wagons. People avoided us, and we left not knowing how many dead or dying there were in Little Rock, Arkansas.

We couldn't tell when we got into Indian Territory; there was not a river, sign, or fence. We crossed the Poteau River and knew we were getting close to our home range. The Sans Bois Mountains hovered into view, and we decided to winter over close to the river. There was not a person in view for weeks on end. We heard all kinds of tinklin' cowbells, and then a small wagon clanged into camp without a driver. Our outriders were the first to glimpse into the wagon and came away with sick hearts. We had been warned by the doctor to not be around anybody, but this had to be looked into. He found two elders, one barely alive, with a young squaw and two children still breathing. I took the old elder in with me and found the old saint couldn't talk. I thought, *Well, the old boy won't last long.*

We buried the dead, set the squaw downwind, and tried to help where we could. The team of mules was so thin, we wondered how they got this far with the Indians aboard. The tinlkin' bells turned out to be several goats that were trained to follow the wagon. The goat herd had free reign to feed along the trail, and we found out the nannies needed to be milked. Much to the joy of all our kids, we had fresh milk. My charge improved with the coming days, and we found out the goats were his. I would set Orville out in the sun where all his goats would come and check up on his health and lay down around their keeper.

Our doctor helped them back to life, and we had another family to feed. Our outriders came with turkeys they had shot; we dined on the larder of the land. Our turn with the smallpox was over, and we started drying jerky as fast as animals were killed. Everybody got involved from the smallest to the oldest, there was a job for everyone. A large hog showed up one day, and we knew we could last the winter if we could catch animals like that.

As our new family grew stronger, we found out she was an accountant from Atlanta, Georgia, and that her husband had died on the trail, the rest of them come down with the smallpox. They were afraid to stop for fear of the robbers that abounded and turned the team loose to take them wherever they wanted to go. It was a miracle that they came to us. "We heard your donkey going 'heehaw,' and the mules came here."

Miss Nell, as we called her, played a guitar, and each evening after supper we had a sing along. Our whole group called me Miner and wanted me to lead the singing; I led the only thing that I knew, hymns. We had not had church or any singing since we left Walnut Grove, Georgia. We called this "Church Praising the Lord."

I had put a large ground cover down on the south side of my wagon and nailed the cover to the bottom. My teepee sat as close to the wagon as I could get it. This at least gave me a nice place to winter over. Our clan strengthened that spring of 1810 as Orville and the boys took over milking the goats. They even cleaned up all the brush that was around the camp. We had a constant milk supply, watching the antics of all kinds of kids, ours and the goats. Those boys kind of took up with me; in fact, they followed me everywhere. Oh well, I enjoyed their banter and had two permanent shadows.

Orville turned out to be Miss Nell's uncle, who had been mute from birth. Miss Nell apologized one day for her family's intrusion into my life, and I felt that she didn't need to feel sorry for me; it was I that needed the company. Nell and I exchanged silly grins and parted company with hot, embarrassed faces.

I feel I must continue this through to its entirety and tell how this experience runs in mine and Miss Nell's life. I had never been married except to that lead mine. Miss Nell had lost her husband to the smallpox scourge, and she and her family had survived to join our troupe. We had been put on the same trail to Indian Territory. Now can you see any reason for us not to continue with the circumstances at hand? Trail life is rough; you don't have any time except to keep moving on. The elders sat in council that evening as we stepped across a bow that made us man and wife on the trail west, January 11, 1810.

Delay

I spent my time pouring over the last scans; the map department was making the changes that put the bridge steel one thousand meters further down the river. I enlarged the scan of my twin brother sitting on Yonder Rock with his smirking smile, as if he knew just what I was going to do next. I spent two days in conference with the camp physician. They ran me through a physical and found a thirty-nine-year-old male Indian with Type A positive blood and all the usual cuts and bruises from a very active childhood. The full-body X-ray turned up zilch. They even had a dermatologist run his rough hands over all, I mean *all*, of my skin. I felt like I had been pinched, pothered, and put upon in the last forty-eight hours.

General Lance had me bring the spirit circle into his labs and the reports came back with "Yep, those are real eagle feathers and raw hide from a buffalo." General Lance tried to get on my case about protected species and all that rot that doesn't apply to aboriginal Indians. He saw me smiling, and we had a cup of coffee to ease the tension. His meeting with Mr. Ables turned out to be a fiasco supreme. General Lance had the map department contact a surveyor that detailed the boundaries of the Indian Treaty as the center of the moving water. I had set the Black Hawk down well outside the disputed line. This brought up the point of the quicksand trap. We rechecked the scans of both trips to the center of the sandbars; the first trip showed my tire tracks set on firm sand. The second set showed water diversion had been made in the sandbar, and the consequence was I set down in the same exact spot and got sucked into the quicksand with my Black Hawk.

My air jockey produced the offending landing gear, and metallurgy spent one hundred thousand dollars testing the metal to check if it held up under stress. Their report was that the Black Hawk couldn't produce enough power to have broken the landing gear. General Lance brought me back into his office, and over coffee he told me the findings. I pouched out my brown lips and said something to the effect of "when you're scared, you can do anything." His laugh made my day, and they dropped all charges.

I couldn't get my brother's look out of my head and, consequently, asked for a meeting with General Lance, the head of Rangers and myself. General Lance granted my request if I would meet with him privately first. I contacted his office and was informed that he was waiting for me to accompany him on his monthly flight time. When I turned into the flight line, there was my air jockey, standing in front of my Black Hawk all fueled up and ready to go. General Lance was strapped in the co-pilot's seat. I right quick got my helmet on and made a flight check, but my air jockey stopped me in mid-stride and handed me a note from General Lance. The note read:

Stop. Don't say a word, Chief Feather. Before you go any further, shut off everything in this eggbeater that even resembles an electronic part. Shut off all switches that resemble a radio, scanner, and recorder. General Lance.

I reread the note again and began to do as the note said; I even turned the computer on and deleted everything that was on this side, then the mainframe same way. The last I turned off was the tower radio, my connection to Fox One. General Lance spoke quietly, "Okay, Chief Warrant Officer Four. I want you to take me to the Cimarron River where you were born."

"With all due respect, sir, I will not fly this aircraft without tuning into Fox One."

"Okay, what can you do in an emergency take off?"

"General Lance, this sounds like an emergency to me. I can call my air jockey to me, and he will land line the tower and inform them we need emergency clearance and can't wait for a repair tech."

"Chief Feather get with the program!"

My air jockey turned as white as any white man, picked up his handheld land line, and informed them of the situation. They immediately gave us clearance as soon as my two thousand hp turbines came on line. I held the warm-up light on, and I could feel both turbines start their slow ascent to power. My air jockey stood by and gave the thumbs-up signal, and we were airborne. We flew speechless until we reached the Cimarron River, and I sat down in the exact spot of the quicksand puddle.

PAT LORETT

"Chief Feather, keep your rpm up, and be ready to take off at a moment's notice." It was then I noticed a very heavy, flat case on the General's lap. He dialed the combination lock, zipped open the case, pulled the spirit circle out, and hung it on the overhead sun visor. He took out a stopwatch and started it, laying it in plain sight. I had my hands full of controls and couldn't do anything else but stand by. Exactly ten minutes later, my twin brother appeared on Yonder Rock, and I could feel the suck of the quicksand start.

"Chief Feather, I think its time to tear up another set of landing gear!" I applied full power, and true to form, the left-side landing gear broke in the same spot and fell off in the quicksand. I hovered at thirty feet as the sandstorm raged on the sandbar. A flock of geese tried to come up under me, and the backwash sent them pounding into the sandbar.

"Chief, turn on all the electronics and take a picture of that nut on that rock." I set my ship on auto hover, took countless pictures, and scanned the whole hillside for every known metal, glass, and composite materials. And, for good measure, I looked the whole thing over with penetrating radar. *I bet my brother will get a good sting out of this.* I wasn't watching him, but General Lance said Sam jumped into the river and swam away from the rock. It was about then the rock exploded into a million pieces, and the shock wave sent my precious Black Hawk up and back at least five hundred meters.

Rock and water fell all around in the river, killed more geese, drained the quicksand pool, and I could see a warning light that Fox One was on the air by this time, trying to contact the general. They had recorded an earthquake in the Cimarron River fault lines, were we involved? General Lance satisfied them and ordered me to fly the river for a mile both ways to film the damage every way that I could. I spent another hour filming, and the Payne County Mounties appeared on the old road. General Lance radioed them that there had been a rockslide down river and everything had settled down to the point we were ready to leave.

General Lance contacted Fox One and said the radio has cleared and we would be back on base within the hour. "Chief Feather, what is the top speed of this aircraft?"

"This aircraft will cruise at 198 miles per hour."

"I'm in a hurry. Let's set a record to Fort Sill."

"Yes, sir!" I thought, *We'll blow the goose feathers out of these turbines.* I set the boost on max, fuel rate was off the scale, and we took my bird toward my pad. I offloaded General Lance on the hospital helipad and saw my air jockey on his truck with spare training wheels for my Black Hawk. I hovered enough for him to make the repairs and set down. As the turbines were unwinding, I hung the spirit circle on its visor and wondered what would be the next trap. I made a download of today's activities and saved the documents for future use. General Lance called a meeting of the top brass and invited his pilot of the day to present our findings.

"Gentlemen, we have had quite a afternoon with a resident of the Cimarron River, Sam Feather, twin brother to Chief Feather, who was my pilot of this latest excursion. I have done the very test of the spirit circle that we discussed in our last meeting. Chief Feather, this will fill you in on the incursion of a top secret listening device."

What else can I get embroiled in, I thought.

"Chief Feather, the other day when I brought that spirit circle into my office, a silent alarm was triggered in security that there was a listening bug. Security came in and found the bug sewed into that spirit circle. They locked it up in a lead-lined case, and a trap was set down on the Cimarron River that you didn't know anything about. I was privy to all the information, and I used you as a guinea pig. Your brother took the bait, and at this very moment my rangers are arresting your brother on several counts of espionage against the United States government. We don't know at the present time all the ramifications of the charges. Chief Feather, you are cleared with top secret clearances from your service in the Iraq and Kuwait wars, and no doubt these clearances will cover the impoundment of your brother. You are not to discuss this information with anybody. Are you clear on this point?"

"Yes, sir, General Lance, but with all due respect to your army rangers, I don't think they can apprehend my brother on his own turf." I could see a storm brewing and was enjoying myself.

"I have access to the most elite Rangers in the world, and they can do this exercise."

"Yes sir, I understand fully."

They don't know my brother. Sam and I had trained together in boot camp. He went on to take advanced training with the Navy Seals. I had gone to the helicopter division and had been checked out on the Black Hawk series. We both served in the Iraq and Kuwait theaters at the same time. Sam wanted more time with his family, I stayed with my Black Hawk, and here we are today on opposite sides.

ORVILLE

My life was always one of seclusion, fraught with doubts about myself. I had lived with my in-laws all my life. Why I couldn't speak, I never knew or even thought about. My family always felt sorry for me, and I just lived with whoever wanted some company. This brings me to my aim in life, listening and nodding my head if somebody wanted to talk to me (which I enjoyed), being quiet, and hearing the news on the wind. I had been taught to sign, and this talent had carried me through sixty-one years of life.

Goats were my best friends in life, and I could supply butter and milk to all my little charges. Yes, I was the built-in sitter for anyone to leave a child, an ailing body, or as I have said, a listener. I awoke from the smallpox scourge with another man in charge of me. The smallpox had taken Nell's husband and made the rest of our wagon so sick we didn't care if we lived or not. My goats were faithful, following us through the wilderness, and the little kids could help themselves to all kinds of milk.

My new keeper was called Miner, and he would tinker with anything; sharpen scissors, a jokester, most of all a singer of chorales and hymns. I loved to hear the old songs that were forever. Nell would play her guitar, I would tend my goats, and it wouldn't be long before we had a singing chorus walking along with the Feather clan. We had another big, fat walker; he was some relation of Miner's and Sara's. Woody, as they called him, was a talker. We would walk along with the wagon or my goats, and he never shut up. As I remember, they called him some kind of a doctor. I never saw him doctor anybody; they must have been wrong.

I wasn't much for riding; so as soon as my strength returned, I would walk along with the loose stock, sometimes bending the brush down so my herd of goats could help themselves to the tender top shoots. Miner and Nell had gotten married along the trail, and I respected their time together. Of course, the wagons could travel faster than Woody and I could walk, so we ambled our own gait, sometimes coming in after dark to join the troupe trailing into Indian Territory. I don't remember when L'ear got to hanging back with me, but she was a free spirit and would lead me anywhere the clan stopped.

I was satisfied with the progress we were making, but that donkey got to acting strange. Run along behind, then charge forward, kicking and doing her hee-hawing to the four winds. Miner got in on the charging act and warned us to watch for outlaws on the trail. The outriders would come back just to check up on us. For all the good that did, didn't save one of my nannies from the sharp claws and teeth of a tawny wild cat.

We heard the fracas start, my herd went in all directions, but it was L'ear that came to the rescue. Mr. Wild Cat didn't pay much attention to a little ole striped donkey until his tail was being chomped! Woody and I witnessed the fray at the moment L'ear started beating the brains out of that ole wildcat on the rocks. Needless to say, the fight didn't last much over five minutes until the cat became a rag. That wasn't near enough for Miss Donkey—she began to maul the bones until all of them had been broken, then stomped the remains into the dust. Finished up her attack with a long drawn out hee-haw. The outriders had come with arrows nocked. We were standing around with our teeth hanging out as a scratched-up nanny came by so fast, it was just a blur.

Oh yes, the nanny lived to be milked again, with long scars across her back, and we sure learned to pay more attention to the guardian donkey. Miner and Nell scolded until they were red in the face. Me? I still couldn't say a word. Woody found out he could walk and talk much faster.

INDIAN TERRITORY

Nell and I started our marriage with Orville and the two boys, living out of my large Conestoga wagon for the next few months. We kept spreading animal fat to seal the bottom of the wagon so it was water tight when going through the rivers.

As soon as we got into Indian Territory, we never saw the militia again. We guessed they thought their job was complete as soon as the Indians were out of sight. We saw many Cherokee clans, but we kept to ourselves and made tracks as fast as we could. The large oak forests hid our clan of Feathers; the only thing that bothered us was that we couldn't see very far ahead. This put the outriders back in use again. Our meat supplies were running low, and the outriders were on the constant lookout for any game.

How did we get into the act of feeding the mass of starving Indians? I guess we had soft hearts and would feed them soup and all the hard bread we could fix. Our outriders brought some stinky antelope that about turned our stomachs. We ate what we wanted and served the rest to anybody that looked hungry. Our guests never complained about the prong-horned antelope we served. One of our college students remembered that wild garlic cooked with wild game made everything more palatable. I wondered where he had been all our trip, but we did develop a taste for any meat our riders killed.

Our guides had scouted ahead and found me an area on the south side of the Cimarron River. We were dreaming about settling down and living our old ways again. We relaxed our guard, and I suppose we felt secure in our surroundings. Nell and I used the Land Patent papers, filed on a parcel of ground from the Cherokee Indian Nation, and were granted a section of land that bordered the Cimarron River on the north. We built our first wooden house that looked like a cone shaped teepee, a step above our wagon with those flapping covers. I knew how to catch fish with my miner's hands, and we had plenty of fish taken from the river.

All the supplies brought from Georgia were divided amongst the clan. I inherited the maps that directed us into Indian Territory. We dispersed among those river bottoms and hills that summer of 1811. We decided to live like the white man. Our transition into the white man's ways was for us to give up all those old Indian superstitions. Our river bluff was riddled with caves that we used to store maps and supplies, and we settled down to learn to farm. I continued to use my ledger. I didn't date each entry, as time didn't seem to matter anyway.

Nell tried to feed the crowds coming by our farm. We had seen hard times before; this was the worst treatment we had seen. The best we could do was make fry bread and beans with some grease, if we had any. I was determined to help our fellow man, and this turned out to be the best way. I had all these lead-covered gold nuggets and couldn't cash them in. I knew if I turned up at a trading post with the nuggets, the word would get out there was gold across the Cimarron. We traded fish for anything to eat at the trading post. We did okay, but the masses were starving.

I was hand fishing in the riverbank one day and ran across an underground cave. Closed places didn't seem to bother me. I held my breath, swam several feet into the riverbank, and come up in a very dark cave. Of course, there wasn't light of any kind, and I gave up for the day. I had a dream-vision that night and could see a hiding place for all my lead-covered gold.

The next day, I put an oilcloth around some firebrands and took them into my newly found cave. As I lit the first one, the sight set me to running. Here were Indian carvings from millennia ago. I couldn't tell when the hieroglyphs were carved, just that they had been set in stone for the ages. My firebrand seemed to flicker, and I discovered there was a draft coming from somewhere. I lit another and discovered there were plenty of firebrands ready to use in the rock face. This led me higher up into the newly found rock edifice. A small room opened up higher in the bank, and I ran at this find. The last resident was still at home, completely dressed, all the bones in their dying position. This was just about more than I could handle. I would have left, but the light ahead caught my eye. I was behind a large sandstone ledge, and the breeze came around the rock.

I mulled this sanctuary around the next day and decided to never tell anybody about the cave, but to gather the bones and bury them the old Indian way. I had a hard time taking hold of the bones, they seemed so light. As I filled his sack, I wondered who the bones belonged to, what kind of life the person had lived. The cloth sack seemed to be the rightful crypt for the rest of the ages. I found a receptacle burial site higher up in the cave and reserved it with the ancients' past.

With this in mind, I started that day to move two tons of lead covered gold into its place in the earth. I don't know how long it took me to completely empty my cache from the wagon. As I've said before, time didn't matter, I had figured out how to disperse the gold. I set up my kiln in the cave and melted the lead slag off the gold and had gold marbles, then ground them to dust and carried a leather pouch with a small pinch of gold to the trading post. Never more than what could be traded for a sack of beans or corn. I always wore old miner's clothes and looked so down and out. The owner of the post called me Trader Joe, and I called him Tex-Mix as we became very good friends and helped each other.

I wrote this entry in my journal started by Woody and plotted out the rest of my life. My aim was to preserve the clans from starvation, and this seemed to fall in place.

SAM FEATHER

Hee, hee, I'll teach that twin brother of mine to not bring his modern flying machine on this holy ground. My quicksand trap could capture the unwary in a heartbeat, swallow evidence by the tons, and nobody will be alive to tell the difference. All I had to do was divert river water into the pit, and instant capture was attained. It took me a month to bury that pipe across the Cimarron River to the sandbar, another six months to drill through Yonder Rock to install the dump valve that diverted river water to the sandbar. It took a track hoe another two weeks to dig a one-hundred-foot-long basin under the sandbar and fill with river sand. The Cimarron River bend area was all abuzz about me out in the river tearing up the sand. They as much told me to my face, "There goes that crazy Sam Feather again, making a mess." The rest was easy. With that six-inch pipe, I filled the pit and the trap was set. All I had to do was sit on Yonder Rock, and my weight would trip the dump valve, and the quicksand pit was loaded in less than ten minutes.

My next project was designing a spirit circle that could be used as a listening bug within fifty miles of my computer. I spent several sleepless nights as one with the spirits—foot and rot; all I did was lose sleep. I finally figured out all I had to do was connect a wire to that ole river bridge steel, and I could listen in on anybody that was around the spirit circle.

That first night, it was a chance meeting with my brother, Lone, at the controls of his precious Black Hawk. Oh, did I enjoy dancing around his camera and messing with the minds of the United States government. I made a joke of all their equipment and had a good laugh. I could hear my spirit circle somewhere out on the flight line all that night and the next day. When that General Lance took it to his office, I thought I would bust. Oh boy, did I have fun with that one. For some reason, my spirit circle must have gone bad, because all I could hear was muffled voices. When the Black Hawk showed up the next day, I thought *I'll show those boys who is in command.* I sat on Yonder Rock and acted my part as a shaman of the Cherokee tribe. My brother, Chief Feather, was a sly one and didn't get into the quicksand enough for me to capture a twenty-million-dollar Black Hawk, but I did get a part of his landing gear. Hee, hee.

That Black Hawk escaped from my trap again, and I felt the first heat rays from its penetrating radar. I knew it was going to get a lot hotter, so I dove into the river and swam into the cave under the bank. Something exploded, and I lost my hearing while under the water. When I came to, I was floating downstream away from Yonder Rock. The Black Hawk was upstream taking pictures of the rockslide, and Yonder Rock was no more. I couldn't figure out what had happened and hid under a logjam until the copter left. Getting back to my cave was pure agony as the world seemed to swim in circles. I knew I needed to hide, and the only thing I could think of was in the cave above Yonder Rock. *Surely this is not the end,* I thought as I made the center chamber.

General Norman Lance

As I have said before, debriefings take as much time as the war, and this was no exception. General Lance and I had witnessed an explosion of considerable magnitude down on the Cimarron River. I had lost more landing gear that was deemed possible and taken several boxes of glossy prints and scans of the complete river bend for two miles. There were films of penetrating radar.

My air jockey had to clean goose feathers from both turbine engines, and the camp rangers couldn't find my brother Sam. Well, no surprise there. They had taken ground samples of the explosion and determined it was TNT in origin. The map department showed a series of caves that was hidden in the river bluffs with no living human occupants. My Black Hawk was grounded pending a complete inspection.

A top-secret meeting was called by General Lance, and we started trying to figure out what happened. All the findings were laid out on the conference tables, and we went well into the night. We were on the second round of coffee when security sirens began to wail all over the base. We didn't have a clue until we looked out on the flight line, and there sat my Black Hawk, glowing an ominous purple. That could only mean one thing: that Black Hawk was radioactive to the tail rotor! Security clamped the base down, isolated my copter away from contact with operations, a detail of protectively-suited personnel came with ultraviolet lamps, and the General and I glowed with the same purple aura.

The baths started within the hour, and we were decontaminated to each hair on our bodies. All this is bad, but the news came from one of the senior doctors. This purple tinge wasn't radioactivity but a dye that usually comes from lead mining. General Norman Lance pulled himself to his full six-foot height. "You mean your department gave me a scrub down for nothing?"

I thought, *You know, we got a free bath General; we won't need to take another bath until Saturday night!*

My general, Norman Lance, was not to let them get by with this. "Okay, doctors, you are so good at decontamination and not checking what the purple was before you scrubbed my hide so thoroughly. Take your team out on the flight line and scrub-a-dub-dub that purple Black Hawk until it shines black again."

I hit the sack and let the brass give my copter a car wash supreme. I was told later it took them the rest of the night, or until my air jockey called them off.

We started getting in results from all the scans that General Lance and I had taken; we discovered a plastic line had been buried in the riverbed, running from Yonder Rock to the sandpit. There must have been a mechanical valve of some kind that controlled water going to the quicksand. The map department scaled out the caves hidden in the rock faces and noted that a small form, like a lead pot, was under the rock debris. The meetings took first place until all the scans were interrupted, pictures were analyzed, and each brass was satisfied that the recon was on United States soil and not on Indian land. Mr. Ables was notified that the rangers were going back to arrest Sam Feather for acts against the United States government. He in turn denied the request and told General Lance that his Indian police would take care of the situation. You should have seen the smoke roll from General Lance's neck, or maybe that was steam.

LIFE IN INDIAN TERRITORY, 1811

I finished unloading all my lead-covered gold nuggets into the Yonder Rock cave. Took the double bottom out of the wagon and started right in building a smaller wagon just like the first. L'ear was in attendance for the complete project, as if she knew when we were going on the road to trade beans. I cut a Bois D'Arc tree and used a drawknife to hew the axles to size. Next, I hewed out the hubs and made the wheels out of the same tree. The tarred boards that came from the wagon went back on the same way they came off. I tarred the bottom and had the same serviceable wagon, only smaller. I even heated the side bows and made them fit. I made shafts and a collar that fit over L'ear's neck, sewed the cover so I could keep everything dry, and was ready for business. Nell made me a bedroll out of an elk hide to use during the cold nights. For some reason that I didn't know about, Nell was sick every morning, then she was okay the rest of the day. I told her that I was going back into the woods to find my clans and try to help them where I could. Nell would pack me all the fry bread she could stack into a cloth bag, and off I would go toward the trading post. I can't remember ever leading L'ear; she would follow me wherever I wanted to go. There were two hounds that liked to travel along, and all four of us set out. Tex-Mix's post was always my first stop to trade for several small sacks of dried corn or beans. We would almost fill my wagon to the top, and that became the measure for a pinch of gold. My Trader Joe name stuck, and I let it be my guise to feed the starving masses. I took along bow and arrows and lived off the land while on the trails.

I began to see the plight of the disposed Indians while making my rounds; I could just see Nell and I in the same well of despair. My first trade while on the trails was a small camp of Delaware Indians. My wagon had begun to squeak, look old, unkempt, and we toddled right into their camp. An old chief, long worn out, greeted me, and I took him a fresh-killed rabbit and enough beans for a meal. We signed to each other, and I knew the six or so people were starving to death. The kids were all sitting around, lifeless for lack of food. We signed, and his squaw came out and gave me an old spirit circle. I giggled kind of crazy-like and give her a complete bag of corn. Their eyes teared over, and L'ear, the dogs, and I moved on before they could kill and eat one of my dogs.

The next stop was closer to a small stream, and as I rattled into the camp, I could smell fish being dyed over an open fire. I never tried to out trade anybody, but a mess of salted dried fish for a bag of beans was an eager trade on their part. This clan was doing better; as L'ear led us over the next hill, I looked back in time to see a long, appreciated wave. My troupe of animals, the wagon, and I made it back to our farm by the river, and I was sure glad to be back in the river to take a bath again. Nell hugged me and showed me her swollen paunch. All I could do was stand and stare, and then she took my hand and put it over our growing child. I didn't sleep much that night, thanking the Lord for the child he was growing inside of her. We hung the spirit circle outside the house and ate the salted dried fish in one meal.

SAM'S GRAVE

I awoke in the night and tried to get into the cave. Chilled to the bone, my head was swollen and ready to explode, and I knew I needed medical attention from drifting in and out of consciousness. All I could think about was how my brother, Lone, had turned the penetrating radar on and Yonder Rock had blown up.

I slept some that night and could just see sunrays coming into the top of the upper chamber. I found blood all over the floor from my ears and knew I wasn't long for this world. I got out my computer, tuned on the spirit circle, and heard muffled flight line noise. I set my cave trap with my computer, listened as my own body noise began to falter, and thought, *Those 155-millimeter projectiles will erase all evidence, and I will get even with my brother.*

NIGHT PATROL

General Lance called me into his inner office and informed me the sprit circle was active again. Security had traced the signal to the flight line. "Now, Chief Feather let's try to locate Sam by his own signaling devices."

"What do you have in mind?" I listened to his plan and agreed: we needed to find Sam before the office of the BIA, namely Mr. Ables.

"I want to go to the Cimarron River with an ultra-violet light and try to locate the source of the reception. Chief, this mission is strictly on the QT. I don't even want my own Fox One to know where we are or what we're going to do. Can your Black Hawk run silent long enough to scan the river banks in the dark?"

"Yes, sir, we will be limited on speed and fuel, but we should have plenty of time."

"Let's do a recon after bed check tonight and get the rangers to disguise us for the occasion."

"General Lance, with all due respect for your rangers, we should disguise ourselves from the Black Hawk's supplies and not tell anybody where we are going."

"Yes, Chief, that is the idea, but Fox One would have his radar scope on to monitor us."

"Yes, but doesn't Fox One need to do a radar checkup tonight?"

"Hmmm, yes, I can see where we would have time to do our snooping around on Indian Land. Okay, we just might get ahead of the BIA this once."

I contacted my air jockey and had my freshly washed Black Hawk refueled and serviced for the night's recon. This time I was determined to get ahead of my own brother. I made my Black Hawk just as the radar screens went blank. As the twin turbines began their ascent to power, I prepared to run as silent as I could. General Lance appeared out of the darkness with his face blacked out and a black suit on. We really were one with the night as we disappeared over the horizon silently.

The flight took over an hour as we ran under any radar that might have been on. I turned on the ultraviolet lamps as we cleared the south bank; our view was a complete violet hillside showing the remnants of Yonder Rock. We could see the origin of the explosion, the remnants of the bottom cave, the hill spring; I set the Black Hawk down well outside of the quicksand pit and unwound all the sounds before disembarking on the sand. We could just see the outline of the riverbanks and headed to Yonder Rock.

There was no need for the ultraviolet lamps, so we used our night vision goggles to show the way. We quick-stepped across the river and hardly got our legs wet. I took out my powder dispenser and every few feet checked for invisible beams of laser light. We crawled into the lower chamber and rechecked again. The general spoke softly about all the lead slag that was piled up along the sides of the cave. We couldn't figure out where all this was going or what all this was about.

As we crawled toward the upper room, I had the feeling we weren't alone. I found the first laser beam about one foot off the cave floor. I knew then my brother was in the cave, too. I puffed more powder and found more beams on up in the cave shafts. I listened to the wind as it wound up the shaft and could hear the wind outside my helicopter and knew that the spirit circle was activated. I hand signaled us to back down and not to make any noise.

I don't get scared too often, but the silence of the cave was getting on my nerves. We did a recon of the immediate area and found lots more lead slag, the lead pot, and some round lead marbles. We took samples of everything and only left our footprints in the purple dye. A return to base reloaded our minds with more questions for the coming day. Fox One identified us as soon as we climbed out of the river bottom. We came back with Lone One clearance, gave an all-clear transmission, and dead-headed to my pad. My air jockey lit the area and signaled with his hand lamp. As the turbines were unwinding, General Lance addressed me as Chief Feather, and we knew we were on the right speaking terms.

"Chief Feather, tonight's recon never happened. Is that made completely clear?"

"Yes, sir. General Lance, I request an immediate briefing to plan our recon this afternoon."

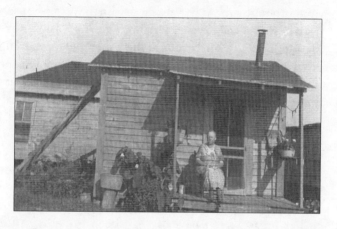

NELL

I made as many visits as I could, trading along the way. I found a map of the Cimarron River area and marked each homestead and teepee in my native scrawl. This turned out to be the best way of keeping track of my peoples. My trading expanded to knives, all kinds of cookware, and a very necessary item, needles and thread. I knew not to buy very much, and Tex-Mix helped me supply my wagon. L'ear turned into the best guard donkey; with her hee-haw and the dogs barking, I was saved many a time from the wild boar that roamed the river bottoms. I memorized all the den trees for squirrels, day and night beds where the hogs hung out, pecans by the wagonloads, and made it home before Nell's time. I had made several trades with my fellow man of jerky, dried fruits, toys for the boys, and a large buffalo robe.

Nell was as big as her clothes would stand. She had been visited by Early Bird, our neighbor, and they made plans for the coming birth. I was a wreck of nerves each time I thought about her giving live birth to another son or daughter! One Feather was born during a large waxing moon; Early Bird brought me a very wet, screaming boy wrapped in his first blanket. I took him down the bluff to my favorite Yonder Rock and gave him his first bath in my hill spring. He settled down in my warm arms and took his first nap under the full moon. All I could do was cry my eyes dry and praise the Lord for bringing us to this new land, showing me a way to sustain our peoples. I prayed for the strength to continue helping my fellow man. I quick-stepped back into our home, just as Nell was cleaned up and eagerly took One to her breast. I felt new life had been brought to the Cimarron River bend and we would survive.

The word got out that I was a crazy trader and what if people took advantage of me—I always took home more than I left, and my family was blessed. There was never a time that my wife and boys was mistreated or were in want for meat. They would find fresh-killed carcasses hanging beside our home and never know who brought them.

Tex-Mix was the only man that knew what I was doing, and he always filled my wagon with more than I bargained for. He was a constant source of information, and I was the carrier. This alliance brought the news that there was a white man disguised as an Indian who was stealing anything he could get his hands on, sometimes beating women into submission. Yes, this Trader Joe got real mad, and Tex-Mix wanted me to carry a gun in my double-floored wagon. I did have a bow and arrow for small game that suited my needs; what I didn't tell was that I had a long Spanish sword in my shallow box, too.

L'ear was the first to warn me that I was being followed, looking around and twitching those long ears.
The dogs gave their growling sounds; the hair stood up
on my neck. I traveled away from civilization; I didn't
want anybody to be involved with what I had in mind.
I started building a big fire at night, rolling my bedroll
up against a rock ledge, sleeping on my spare blanket
on top of the ledge. I scented my outlaw before dark
and set my trap with my sword at hand.

It was one of those nights, almost dark, no wind,
and L'ear could hear for a mile. My dogs and I lay in
our place on top of the ledge, and I saw a giant creeping silently in against the skyline. His shot ruffled my
empty bedroll. As he was trying to reload his musket,
the dogs tore his shirt completely off; he parried with
a knife and slashed open the rib cage of one of my
dogs and went for the other. L'ear got into the fray and
kicked the knife outside of the fire light, turned, and
took her first bite out of the outlaw's leg. This gave my
other dog the opportunity to cut one of the old scoun-
drels' hamstrings, and there lay the outlaw, squealing
like a pig. I thought to myself, *you know, Miner, there
isn't any need for me to get blood on my hands. I think I'll
sit this one out.*

I didn't sleep any that night, but the cries of the
bandit grew thinner and shallower. I stayed out of sight
until he bled completely out, and I had thoughts of
moving on and let somebody else find this mess. Yes,
that became my plan, I packed up all my belongings,
brushed all the tracks out, sewed up my dog with donkey hair, and headed on down the river to visit somebody else. I felt remorse for a while as to what had
happened, but I had to see my mission through and got
on with life.

I just had to travel back to my Nell, the boys with their little brother, and spend some moons enjoying them until that ole traveling feeling came back again. My dog healed up, and L'ear settled back to her ole normal cranky self. My journal was swelling from the trips, and I began to trust L'ear to find all the different tribes. It was unerring how that donkey could smell out the downtrodden. All I had to do was follow the wagon and she could find when one was sick or out of food. Many a night we traveled the back trails and I couldn't see a hand in front of my face, but she would lead me back in the oak woods to another unknown settlement. One other thing that always amused me: she would start to bray a long way from each settlement, and if they had any horses, they would answer with a bugle call. I would be met halfway with the latest news. One night, L'ear left me and didn't come back for two days. This scared me until I got the smell of my donkey. I took her out in the river, washed all the old donkey smell and thought, *Well, well in a few months I can expect a little L'ear!*

There was one thing about the Indian tribes that were dispersed into Indian Territory. I know I was scared to talk to anybody about the age before the dislodgment when we came over in 1810. Most tribes thought we had done something wrong and that was why the United States government forced us into exile. I was able to travel unopposed into the areas of greatest need. I never asked for help and never was offered any. Of course, the word never went out in the Indian territories that there was any help for the Indians. Tex-Mix at the trading post helped me furnish seeds to the ones that would try to farm. Most of the corn, beans,

squash, and seeds of all garden vegetables were found
in my supplies from the post.

I never kept track of the goods that I spread to the
masses; I only knew the peoples were improving their
lives. Oh yes, there were the old hardheads from the
land down south that was not going to improve their
ways. They never tried to learn the language or farming
of the white man, and they soon had their dead bodies
up in the air for the birds to pick clean. All I could do
was try to help by letting the tribes take advantage of
me and go off mumbling to myself. I never told anybody of my gold cache or where I melted it down; Yonder Rock became my secret hiding place for the age.

Mr. Anthony Ables

The pain in the backside, Mr. Ables, always seemed to come at the wrong time for me to get very much done. General Lance and I had made plans to ferret out my brother from the caves. We knew the spirit circle was activated, the cave was fortified with explosives, and here came Mr. Ables. A quick-called meeting put the BIA, me, and the general in the same meeting room. General Lance recognized Mr. Ables and asked him what he had in mind. I could see he was still miffed about not getting to use his men to arrest Sam Feather. *Ah, good, the ole boy is still one trip behind us; he doesn't know we have been back down there.*

Mr. Ables rambled on and on about this was Indian land, the original land patent was still in the Miner Feather's estate, and he was the custodian of the grant, and yada, yada. More legalities about Sam Feather was the present heir and we were trespassing on private land. I was wanting to take a nap and snapped to my best wide-awake thoughts—I did the linage of the Feather clan, and I was next in line for that old land grant! *If Sam is dead, I could file on 640 acres of the Feather clan holdings and have it in my hands before day's end.* Lucky for me, Mr. Ables ran down and said his goodbyes just in time. I told General Lance the line of linage, and the light in the deer eyes come on!

"Chief Feather, I want you to meet with my department of rangers and plan a recon to find all those explosives. Bring your brother, if he is still alive, here under arrest. I want his computer and all equipment that is connected with the spirit circle. I know what you think of my rangers, but they are the best to be had. I want you to fly them down on the Cimarron River and command the operations, which means I want you to be able to come back here under your own power. I feel it is a matter of national interest to have all of Sam Feather's knowledge gathered for our defense department."

"Yes, sir, I will need an advanced MASH unit to stand by, a bomb squad to handle old explosives, and enough military police to cordon off the section of land."

I wonder what Mr. Ables would give to come on this exercise.

SICKNESS

Hardly a trip was made that I didn't find sickness by the score, and I made a habit of coming toward the camps from up wind. L'ear would give her bugle call, and there would be someone to come out to meet me. If there were sickness in the camp, I would leave a bag of whatever and go on with my trip. As the general health improved for the immigrants, my appetite was sated beyond imagination. I always ate whatever was in the stew bags with no questions asked. This started my jerky trading; I've eaten the best, fed my dogs the rest, wondered what kind of an old donkey the meat had been taken off of, and never complained one word. This got me to acting my part by mumbling along the trails. Now don't judge me too quickly; this was my way of feeding the tribes around us. Only the elders and shaman realized the truth; they gave me protection that I needed to scour the countryside openhanded.

L'ear grew to the size of a small, fat horse before she delivered me a male copy of herself. I was glad I was home, because she sure needed Early Bird's help. Nell and the boys gentled the little sprite to follow me around. My days of traveling all over the country was solved by L'ear herself. When that sprite grew hungry, he could find his mother wherever we were. This added another travel animal, and I grew to trust them all the more.

I began to feel hot, slow, thirsty out on some trail that I couldn't remember. We made camp by the Cimarron River, and I fell into my Elk hide blanket. The days came and went. I only remember the dogs sleeping with me and me being so hot, I awoke several times and my only thought was getting home to my family. I remember getting in the wagon and moving along the trail. I needn't have worried. L'ear took me home to my family on the river. L' ear must have traveled day and night, and as Nell woke up one morning, she could hear that donkey's long, drawn-out hale. Nell sent one of the boys for Early Bird, and they got me to bed. I awoke in a couple of days, much relieved. Early Bird said I had colic and wanted to hold me on her knees. I thought I'd rather be colicky than suffer a night stretched out on her knees. I hove to and got on with my mission. Sick or no, I had to get away from that.

Thief Jake

Don't move Jake. Don't move a muscle. This ole trapper was famous for talking to himself and had gotten out of many a bad spot. Indians were after his hide, and they had good reason—he had stolen several religious pelts, sacred bows, and above all, the tribe's women. Ole Jake, a wiry trapper that dressed like the locals, headband with rawhide thongs; long, knee-length moccasins; with a certain brown color of the Mexicans. He had walked in with the disposition of the Indians from Florida and found a fertile ground to steal for a living. He made his usual noisy approach to throw them off guard and to look at their camp of several teepees scattered along this sandy red river. His first contact was aimed at the appearance of a trader of furs, stay a day or two, move on to the next bend of the river and try to find a good stand of oaks among the rock bluffs. *Yep, thar she is,* he told himself. *Wonder what's over the hill, hmmm, more oaks, a perfect getaway path,' twill suit me perfect.*

Indians who were trying to winter over on this turn in the river always furnished plenty of winter game, fish, wood—even small bands had passed by to trade, swap hand signals, even trade horses. This winter a new passerby had come, traded some, and ambled on up the red sandy. It wasn't till the next moon that precious goods were missing there and over in the next valley, such as religious wraps and some bows that had existed forever. A quickly-called council as to who had passed through the camps proved that Ole Jake was the only one different!

Jake relaxed as the small band went out of sight around the river to that bunch of river rocks. *Oh well,* mused Jake, *I'll hide the loot and maybe find another band across the river.* The cliff rocks furnished his favorite spot between boulders, all grown up with buck brush to leave his plunder. *Careful in this sand, Jake, don't tear the grass up, wrap all the bows in a buffalo hide, stuff the whole parcel in under the roots so rain won't wash them out. There now, mind mark that spot so you can come back later when those Indians have moved on North for the summer. Hmmm, looks good. On to the next camp.*

Miner heard on the wind how somebody was stealing the tribes of their food; killing and molesting women; and taking precious bows, arrows, and religious buffalo robes. The Indians were poor enough, and now they were destitute. Not to be detoured, L'ear and Miner kept finding Indians that were starving to death. Sometimes they would stay a few days and leave much more than he took in trade. A trip to the trading post put the word out that somebody was doing mischief. Tex-Mix told Miner to not interfere, that the tribes would find the outlaw. It was if Miner had not heard a word as he trudged about his self-appointed rounds.

Ole Jake heard the shot ring out in the morning dew. Always on the lookout for a free meal, his senses sharpened; the first sound was a buck limping out in the clearing and then more sounds of someone tracking the quarry. Ole Jake sighted the hunter, and a single shot from his Kentucky Rifle killed a very young brave. Jake pulled the brave up in a patch of buck brush and laid the brave's rifle so it looked like the boy had shot himself. Jake's next duty was tracking the wounded deer. He knew the deer wouldn't get too far and found the carcass by the Cimarron River. Not one to take too much time with someone else's kill, a quick slash with his machete and both hinds were his to clean at a future time. Ole Jake threw the rest of the deer in the river and was on his way. No regrets, no feelings, do whatever it took to survive.

Miner saw the floating deer that afternoon, minus the hinds. *This can't be right—if an Indian had shot the deer, he would use the complete carcass.* Miner was headed downstream, and it wasn't long before the clean-up birds showed him the body of the young brave. Going on over the next hill, he found the camp of the boy brave. They returned to the dead boy. The mourning started that would last for three days. Miner mumbled to himself, "I bet that killer is still around."

Ole Jake dressed the hinds and was anticipating a roast haunch of deer before dark. A quick slice found a flattened metal ball that glowed in the sunlight like gold! His own mumblings soon brought out the tirade. "Where did that Indian get the precious metal? How can I get the rest of it?" Jake completely forgot about the roast, flew into a rage, and planned to go back to the killing ground as soon as the sun was up.

Reason set in, and Jake had another look at the flattened ball. There was gold covered with lead, and the Indian brave had shot the ball through a Kentucky Long Tom Gun. "I bet the boy didn't know the gold was there," he mused. Ole Jake pondered the subject as he ate his roasted deer. "Somebody out there is making gold-covered lead balls that can be fired through any fifty-caliber rifle."

Miner smelled the outlaw's roast long before he arrived. L'ear sounded off her usual bugle call from up on the hill. Ole Jake was ready long before a little ole man shuffled into camp. *Oh foot,* thought Jake, *it's just Trader Joe and his donkey! Oh, well we can at least trade lies tonight.* Jake served up deer on a stick, and ole Trader Joe ate like this was his last meal.

Miner thought, *I wonder if this Mexican is the outlaw that is killing people. I wonder if this outlaw has figured out the gold covered with lead. I will put out a test and we will see. I'll let one of my marbles fall out of my pocket and see his reaction.* He made sure that Ole Jake was looking and dropped the lead ball in the dust and went to his small wagon like he was getting his bedroll.

Ole Jake could hardly believe his eyes. *That little ole trader dropped one of his lead balls; I will have to bite into it and we shall see. Gold!* I grabbed my machete and attacked the little drawn-up man. I aimed too high and just cut the top off of his hat. I tried to recover and felt the sharp point of a sword slide between my ribs with the strength of a fully-grown man. My arm fell loose, and the machete clattered on the rocks. I couldn't believe I had been out clashed by a runt. My life's blood gushed around my body as I lost all feeling; my last sight was a little ole man standing beside his wagon, waiting calmly for me to bleed out.

Trader Joe stooped, recovered his lead ball, took another bite of the roast deer, took the outlaw's machete, inserted it into the wound, and was satisfied that it looked normal. Brushing his tracks, he left the body for the birds to have their feast. As stories go, the killings stopped, Miner was still making his rounds, Tex -mix knew the difference, several of the religious pelts were found in the cracks of the boulders, and life kept creeping along.

ORVILLE'S VISION

We were home in Indian Territory. As Miner and Nell
settled in on their section of land, I set up camp on up
the river with my own teepee that would let my goats
come and go as they pleased. Nell would come with the
boys, bring bread, and talk to me, and I sent the boys
home with butter and all the milk they could drink.

The first I knew that Miner had become a traveling man; here he came with L'ear pulling a small, two-
wheeled wagon that he had made. He traded me a bag
of beans for a jug of goat's milk. I would have given him
more, but he just mumbled and went on up the river.
I thought, *I wonder where he is going.* In a few days, I
heard L'ear give her bugle call and in strolled the little
ole man a chuckling to himself. "Oh, Orville, look at
what I traded for." All I could see was a bag of jerky,
some fresh greens, and knives that needed sharpening.
He refilled his jug with fresh milk, got butter, and off
he went toward Nell.

The very next time he came through with the wagon filled to the brim, I signed to not let those Indians trade all his corn and beans away. He muttered did I have a nanny that he could borrow? I let him lead my spare nanny, and off he went behind the wagon with the ole boy muttering to himself. I wonder who the crazy one is. Some days later, here he came with an empty wagon and shared his trade goods with me. I signed about the nanny, "I left her with a needy family that had a lot of kids." He had delivered the sharp knifes, traded for a hind of deer, a hide rug that he left with me, and wandered off singing some ole chorale. This became the norm for Miner Feather to trade with the Indians along the Cimarron River. I was getting too old to milk very many goats, so he loaned them out to the different clans. Sometimes they would come back kind of poor, but I let them have free reign to all the foliage along the river, and they soon slicked up.

We had never counted the years in our clan. You knew when to get old, and nobody had to tell you were getting wrinkled, slow, stooped-shouldered, and smooth-mouthed. Your feet were way down there; you had to scratch your back on a close-by tree; then the most aggravating, I forgot. Oh yes, it's time to go to bed and the sun just came up. My first journey into the vision world came quite unexpectedly, while I was napping! Scared me spit less, I had sat outside under a shade tree and fell over in the soft sand and had me a good old-fashioned nightmare. The sun was down, wind was blowing, and I was so cold, I couldn't even get back into my teepee. The apparition started in the river water, spread out over where I was setting, poof! it was gone. I had never had a chance to ask if it was after me or someone else. Next day, same time, same vision, same results.

The next day, Miner came and I tried to sign him my dreams. "Orville, it's okay, you are getting old, and the ancients are suppose to dream dreams. You just let it happen and tell them to me." I squinted my eyes at that runt and retired to my pallet with my four-legged friends.

So help me, I couldn't get the vision out of my head. You just bet every day during one of my dreams the drifting vision would come out of the water. Sometimes it would slap me on top of my bald spot, then split into a vapor that drifted off.

I thought I was losing my mind until here come Miner in from one of his trips with blood dripping out from under his floppy hat, weak as a kitten and talking out of his head. I got his clothes off, sewed a big flap of skin back on the very top of his head, washed the blood down the Cimarron River, and put him to bed in my teepee. Washed his buckskins in the river until they were soft and clean. I about burned his floppy hat, but the only thing that was wrong with it was the top crown was hanging down. I turned the hat wrong side out and took all one day to stitch it together. I would get broth and goat's milk down Miner, and he would go off on one of his daydreams just like I had been doing. I stopped having nightmares. My visions were about Miner, not me!

Miner came around in time; it was like he couldn't remember what had happened. I gave him his clothes and floppy hat, and in a few days he wondered off one afternoon like nothing was amiss. I got back into my old habit of taking naps. To tell the real truth, I was dreaming that the Lord took me home and I left all my nannies for someone else to milk.

Praise the Lord!

L'ear's Last Pull

We had to name L'ear's foal and tried several names. My little boy child came up with Big'ear, and the name stuck. I could see L'ear was getting old by this time, so I cut out a bigger wooden collar for Big'ear and tied him to L'ear. We had several wrecks from those flying hoofs, but the association with the shafts put him in a tantrum. He wouldn't stand for these wooden shafts along his sides. I thought, *okay, you young sprite, I'll make a set you will have to wear all the time.* I put his collar on; that fastened the shafts on each side real snug.

Big'ear hated anything that hit his feet, and his legs would rather stand trembling than try to kick the wooden shaft. L'ear took just so much of his resistance, reached over, and took a good bite of his front leg. Oh, cry, whimper, limp, and act sick, that single striped donkey was such a mess of hurt that his own mother would bite him. As I remember to this day, he never acted up while in the shafts. L'ear lasted the summer out, and

I found her under a white oak tree, stone cold dead thirty-seven years after she was born. I cried my eyes out the day I buried her. She was my answer to helping the down-and-out of the Indian tribes that came over the Trail of Tears.

With no donkey to pull the wagon, watch out over me, and warn the clans of us coming, I could have crawled back in the darkest recesses of Yonder Rock and nobody would have ever found me. I sat on Yonder Rock for a day and a night and discovered the secret of the hillside. I could hear my family playing just behind me, no, there was this steep rock. I took a gambling run up the shallow path and found the boys playing stickball on the mesa. This can't be right—it was a long walk away and down on the river bottom. I restaged to Yonder Rock and could hear the playing again. Yonder Rock was a sounding rock for the entire upper mesa! I forgot all about L'ear and started searching inside Yonder Rock and found an old, spider-filled tunnel entrance behind the bones that I had stashed.

My miner instincts took over and led me to the crypts of the ancients, rooms filled with hide bags of— what else—but the bones of peoples past. I could not count or see them for the lack of light. I left that day with the knowledge that the bones were well hidden, and I needn't tell either. My return to the outside world was one of respect for this plateau of the past. My problems of losing L'ear seem trivial compared to the magnitude of the discovery of Yonder Rock's secrets.

My all-time good answer for a deep-seated problem was taking a nap. Nell found me that day lying on Yonder Rock with that smile that only a father can harbor. She sat with me and discovered the sounds of a stick ball game up on the mesa. A smile transformed her face into a glowing symbol that all husbands love, one of peace. The boys soon joined us, and I savored the moment, still needing a donkey to pull my wagon.

I palled at the thought and had no answer until the next day. There was Big'ear standing by the wagon shafts with his collar still on his neck. I thought, *you don't suppose that young stud wants to pull my load*. There was only one way to find out. L'ear was out of the way, and he stepped between the shafts. I took off the training ones and fastened the real ones in their rightful place. I expected an explosion of wagon, donkey, and shafts, and here he stood like, *come on, Trader Joe, let's get on with life*. I couldn't believe my eyes. Here was an untrained stud donkey, ready to show me the clans that needed help.

I did stay one more day with my family and then got on the trail as before. Oh, we had a few rough spots that would spook the unwary, but we were able to get on with my mission. Even my closest friends didn't know the difference with ole Big'ear pulling the load.

Miner Travels

I began to smell, hear, feel Big'ear being spooked. My
dogs kept close by as we camped by the ole red muddy
river. By morning, we couldn't stand the stench. The
red water had turned even darker; we couldn't imagine who stirred up the water. With a full wagon, I was
headed up river to visit some of the Iowa tribe to trade
jerky. I didn't need any, but they needed corn.

The Cimarron River was not drinkable water, and
we had to go up to one of the feeder creeks. We walked
into a settlement called Mulhall. All the teepees were
vacant, horses were tied out to the trees, no dogs, no
women and kids. The fire pits were still warm, and the
smell was worse than ever. Whatever was making the
smell was coming with the southwest winds along with
sounds of cattle; I don't mean a few cows, but thousands. I helped myself to morning jerky and followed
the Indian tracks upwind; this led me to the Cimarron

River and the biggest cattle roundup that I had ever seen.

Indians were up to their elbows dressing out beef to make jerky. I got my knife sharpening equipment, and we soon were in the business of field dressing all the cows that we wanted. We spread hides on the ground and had the horses drag the choice beef to camp. I sharpened all the knifes that we had. The wagon master saw what I was doing and brought all his knifes, and I trundled my stone wheel all day. I shared my corn for the meals, and we ate all the roasted beef that we could hold.

I had stumbled upon the eastern cattle drive of the Chisholm Trail. The trail boss said there were about thirty-six hundred head of Texas Longhorns headed for the eastern markets. The Cimarron River had real steep banks, and several head of Longhorn cattle had fallen off the bank, broken bones, sprained hips, calves had lost mothers, then the final straw: a pet bull was missing. The trail boss got all the Indians around his campfire and told us to help ourselves to the cattle they left; the cattle drive had to move on as soon as the grass was cropped. He asked me where I was from, and I told him on down the river about two days walk.

"Miner, my cook wants to trade you for all the corn and beans you have left in your wagon. What will you trade?"

"Mr. Trail Boss, we need all the cattle you can spare. I can go to the trading post for more corn and catch up with you before you get to the Kansas border." I made a trade that day for all the calves and cattle that were trail-weary or injured.

I would have made good time, but I found the missing Longhorn bull down river after a good day's travel. I hardly recognized the poor brute from all the cuts, bruises, and one missing horn. The trail boss had warned me not to trust their pet bull, because he may have gone mad and would try to hook us with his horns. Big'ear started in with his braying he-hawwww, and wonders never cease to amaze me. This ole bully answered back. I don't get scared too often, but this was eerie, a ton of bull coming to meet us a-limping along. I tried to hide, outrun, act bigger than my three-foot-eleven, but nothing was going to detour a one-horned bull from following us on the trail east.

We stayed clear of each other at first, and I found a friend that wanted company while moving along. I rubbed him down and found he had a stick stuck in between a set of hooves that would cover a dinner plate. Of all the pets that I ever had, this was the best: a full-grown Longhorn bull (with one horn) and a runt of a man holding up the front leg, prying out the hurt. All Bully did was grunt and bleed all over the ground. I took rawhide and bacon grease and bound up the foot, and we went on down the trail. I discovered that Bully (yes, that is what I named him) must have been trained to be in a yoke. All I had to do was put any kind of rope around his neck, and he would walk right along with Big'ear.

We got on the way to the trading post at the crack of dawn with my new pet of the day. Tex-Mix couldn't have been more surprised at my find. I let all the gawking people wonder at what that crazy Trader Joe had to giggle about. Bully and Big'ear stood side by side as we refilled my wagon and stayed overnight so Tex-Mix and I could get caught up with our gossiping. I let my stock graze the back lots, and we left the next morning. I should have charged Tex-Mix for mowing the grass and the fertilizer that Bully left in piles, but I left well enough alone.

The trail boss said to follow the tracks. They were headed to Caldwell, Kansas, with the steers and on north with the breeding stock. I caught up with the herd at Deer Creek just before they crossed into Kansas Territory. They had found plenty of water and graze, and had decided to spend time fattening up the Long-horns. I walked into their camp with a frayed rope around Bully and a small, one-stripe donkey pulling a two-wheeled wagon loaded to the brim with beans and corn and all three-foot-eleven of a Cherokee Indian.

"Ferdinand, its good to see you, you old scoundrel!" came from the cook. Bully promptly broke loose and went to the cook wagon and stood beside the tongue while the cook petted his favorite bull.

"Miner, where in the world did you find Ferdinand?" asked the trail boss.

"That bull found me the next morning on the trail to the trading post. He was all buggered up and had a split hoof with a stick wedged in between. I got the stick out, and he has been with me ever since."

"Please, just call me Boss. We came from Texas, and we haven't learned Mr. yet."

"Okay, Boss, I have had a time showing that ton of bull to everybody on the trail. I don't think anybody had ever seen a Longhorn bull before."

"No, ole Ferdinand is one of a kind. In fact, come with me and I will show you a cow that matches him."

"Cookie, come call your cow." Ole Cookie picked up a frying pan and started beating on the bottom with a big spoon. Ferdinand looked big, but his twin sister ambled up and stood by for Cookie to put a huge yoke over their necks. All I heard was a clicking coming from his mouth, and the pair moved over and stood astraddle the wagon tongue, ready for the day's travel. Yes, I had to admit that Sue was the bigger of the two, and Boss started the telling about Ferdinand and Sue.

"Cookie, Ferdinand, and Sue worked in the hill country of west Texas, pulling logs to a sawmill. Ole Cookie got hurt, and that put those three out of a job. I hired all of them to cook on this trail ride getting these Longhorns to market. We did alright until we got to the Cimarron River, and that wreck separated this trio until now. Miner, I shore owe you for finding ole Ferdinand, and we will repay you somehow. What do you need?"

"I can tell you are a Christian man. Can I give you something, and you not tell where it came from?"

"Miner, I will give my word that not a word will be told about this meeting."

"Okay, I want you to give your wounded or lame animals to the Indian tribes you meet on the trail. We have a saying that a hungry man can't hear. I want you to feed my peoples and then tell them the Lord loves them. Now Boss, I want to pay you for all the animals that you give away. Take these lead marbles, cash them in, keep the money, or give it away to help us survive these times."

"This lead is not worth much, but if that is what you want to do, that's fine with me."

"You don't know the full story. Let's take a walk over yon hill. I want to show you something."

A short walk took us out of earshot, and Boss took a good bite of the lead marble and couldn't imagine what he saw. Then he realized what I was doing to help my peoples. "Miner, your secret will never be known until you are gone; I will do as you say and help your fellow man."

I left the trail ride to the cowboys that day and headed back to my home on the Cimarron River. I had a lot of fun with Ferdinand, but that was way too much bull for me.

STAGING THE CIMARRON

I took a contingent of rangers headed up by Chief Camble to the Cimarron River and sat down on the sandbar up river from the quicksand. We had to find Sam dead or alive before we could proceed with any investigation. General Lance was adamant about using them. "Chief Feather I want you to survive these operations at all cost!"

I briefed the platoon and warned them Sam was a deadly man—he always felt if he had to die to prove a point, then so be it. We set up field radios. They took their carbines and equipment and waded across the river. My thoughts ran like the wild winds that always blew over the hillsides. My Fox One radio sprang to life. "Lone One, we have a delayed analyses from the chemical labs on the type of explosives used in the explosion on what you call Yonder Rock."

"Is this information top secret?"

"Negative, Lone One, this message is from General Lance. He wants you to know what you are dealing with. The message reads as follows: 'Explosive used was TNT. In the amount used in a 155-millimeter projectile, there were trace amounts of base metals used that indicate a fully armed M109 HE, used principally for fragmentation and blast effects."

I did shudder with this last bit of information. I started to radio the Rangers, but pulled myself together and used a signal mirror instead. There might be more 155 shells lying around that would have obliterated the whole site! A courier came back. I told him the news; he told me that yes, there was a dead person in the upper chamber, they were taking movies of the interior and would be back as soon as the area was filmed.

All I could do at this time was remember that all of my family was dead now, except me. I called Fox One and requested a secure channel to General Lance.

"Lone One, this is General Lance on secure channel number four."

"General, the rangers have found a dead body in the upper channel, and I request a full company of military police to secure the section of land we are on. They should stay away from the immediate area. I suspect there are more 155 projectiles buried in the rubble."

"Request confirmed; they will be arriving in one hour one mile south of your area."

"General Lance, start the paperwork to bring Sam Feather's service record to your office. We need to see if Sam was ever involved with 155 projectiles."

"Lone One, as soon as the MP's have arrived, we need to have a top brass meeting in my inner office. Stand by until they have gotten a definitive answer and contact me when you are advised."

"Yes, sir, standing by."

I dreaded hearing the news and was not surprised when the squad showed me the prostrate body of Sam Feather in a pool of dried blood. I called General Lance to have Sam declared dead and to move ownership to me, Lone Feather, ASAP.

Chief Camble continued with, "Your brother is not all our camera showed us. Look at the computer wired up to the detonators, laser lights, and sound detectors in the cave. We need to know where the power source, microphones, and motion detectors are located."

"What you see is all that I know, except the service records of Sam Feather are being assembled by General Lance at headquarters as we speak."

"Chief Feather, I'm sure you want to run inside those caves up on the hill, but we are sure it's impossible unless we can turn the power off to its computer, and then we have to wait until the battery runs down."

"Okay, Chief Camble, load your men. We are going to try to secure the area until we are relieved by the military police." I flew the contingent of men around the section and placed them in sight of each other. It was then we noticed electric power coming to that section of land. Chief Camble noted this; we met with the military police and secured the area. I flew the rangers back to base and could feel the experience weighing in on my shoulders.

General Lance was in conference with whom else but Mr. Ables. I felt it important, made myself known, and was waved into the lion's den. From the looks on those two faces, it wasn't going to be a good day. "Chief Feather, please come in and explain to this civilian the situation of the Feather property on the Cimarron River."

I tried to interject the subject, but Mr. Ables let me know in no uncertain terms that the United States government was trespassing on BIA land. Furthermore, I didn't have any cause to be flying those infernal machines on this holy ground. I let the ole boy run down, sit down, and catch his breath. General Lance produced the quitclaim deed, the original land grant from the United States government made by Miner Feather in 1812, the linage line, pictures of today's excursion, and pictures of my dead brother with all the detonation fuses glowing like a Christmas tree. General Lance and I savored the moment. I forbade him to go on my land and dismissed him. Silence ensued as Mr. Ables packed his brief and made for his car.

General Lance commented, "I don't believe we have heard the last of the BIA or Mr. Ables, Chief Feather."

"General Lance, I know Mr. Ables is headed to the Cimarron River. Let's let the MP's arrest him and have him cool off for a day or two before we call the Bureau of Indian Affairs. This will buy us enough time to defuse this mess in the caves. Then we can start proceedings to lock up the complete area in question."

"Chief Feather, will you do the honor of informing my staff to do as we agree."

"General, it would be a pleasure." Oh, did I like that job. For once in my career, I felt I was completing a task.

"I'm truly sorry that your brother had to die from the explosion on your land."

"I'm sorry that my brother has caused the United States government so much grief. I used to hate the government and for which it stands, but I grew out of that hate at an early age and want to get on with life.

I believe that Chief Camble can handle the situation with the bombs, and I request that you send them back in a Humvee and a six-by-six truck to take over clearing the area. In time, they will call a medical examiner for the body of Sam. I think they should do a complete autopsy, and that will give me time to make the arrangements for a military funeral in my own graveyard."

"Chief Feather, you are dismissed until after the funeral, and I will see to it that all is done properly."

I drove into Lawton, rented a room, took a good hot shower, and went into a dead-dog sleep. Must have slept the clock around, took another shower, and just couldn't get Sam out of my mind. He had served so faithfully until two years ago and went off the deep end after that. I still had the gold-lead marbles to roll around in my pocket. For some reason, all this had to tie together. As I packed up, I got to singing some ditty and found myself heading back into the fray.

Big'ear

My stud donkey was a welcome addition to my aim in life. As I grew older, my gait grew much slower and more unsteady. Oh, I could still trade the necklace off of the Indian maid and make them feel they had gotten the best of this ole trader. I still had plenty of gold-lead marbles and spent my spare time melting lead and grinding the gold to powder. Each melting session seemed to bother me, and I couldn't think as clearly as before. Everything seemed to take longer and was more difficult to do.

Nell had raised the boys to grown men. I had thought about taking some of the family with me, but they were all so bashful scouring the countryside for the down and out, they wouldn't go. I discovered that my new donkey knew his way around as good as L'ear, and I never had a rope on him of any kind. I tried him a time or two, and he would go home the same ole way, slow, you know, just above stop. Tex-Mix at the post was getting old, and we would trade stories till the wee hours of the morning. I would get into my wagon and cover up with my hides and any dog that was along. I have woken several times with Big'ear braying his head off for Nell to come get me out of the wagon.

I felt my mission was almost at an end and had just made it inside my cave when a sharp pain started under my left arm that left me speechless. The world turned completely and left me lying on my back in the upper cave. I got my journal and made my last entry that day. I praised the Lord for letting me live this long and helping our people. August 20, 1863. I put my journal in its place, got ready for my body to start its last long nap, and for me to ever be with the Lord.

Getting Started

The autopsy seemed like it took forever. I wanted to get back to flying my Black Hawk; no news was coming from the Cimarron River. General Lance and I had a daily meeting, and the results came in from the autopsy while we were in session. I opened the sealed envelope, and I know my jaw fell open. General Lance spoke quietly. "I can step out of the office if that will help."

"General Lance, you need to read this letter."

"Oh my good gosh, you didn't kill your brother."

It was if a weight had been lifted off of my shoulders. "I didn't kill my brother" was all that I could say. General Lance grabbed the door and demanded that the courier return. The young sergeant stood at attention until we told him to rest easy, we just wanted some answers.

"Sergeant Wayne," said the general, "who else knows about this letter?"

"Sir, the envelope was sealed. I don't know what was in the letter. The medical examiner gave me the envelope with the instructions to deliver it to your hands only."

"Okay, Sergeant Wayne, who was the ME?"

"Sir, I don't know. He is a civilian called in from Lawton, Oklahoma. He is still in the exam room. If you want, I can go get him."

"Yes, Sergeant, you do just that."

General Lance and I were making plans for the next day when Sergeant Wayne appeared with a little ole wizened man who was out of breath. Sergeant Wayne introduced the ME as Doctor Brithen. So help me, I felt sorry for the little ole guy. He was so out of breath, and I bet he had never seen a real live general before. The general sized up the situation and spoke quietly. "Sergeant Wayne, you are dismissed. We can handle this problem."

"Doctor Brithen, thank you for coming to see me. I hate to bother you, but we have a delicate situation here, and I need to know for sure that you wrote this autopsy for Sam Feather."

Doctor Brithen adjusted his glasses and reread the letter and said in a high falsetto voice, "Oh yes, this is Sam Feather's autopsy. He died of extreme lead poisoning. I've seen a few cases, but this is the worst ever. His lungs were completely full of lead dust, smoke, and some kind of purple dye that I'm not familiar with. It's toxic under high heat. The X-rays of Mr. Feathers' bones were completely saturated with lead salts, his brain stem was full of heavy metal—oh, he had some other minor cuts and bruises, his ear drums were blown out. Probably from an explosion when he was underwater, and it wouldn't have done him any good to eat. His digestive tract was—"

"Oh, oh yes, that will be sufficient, Doctor. I think I understand," quaked the general. "Can you determine how long Mr. Feather was exposed to lead?"

By this time, Doctor Brithen was in his element, touching his fingers together and blowing on them. "Oh yes, Mr. Lance, the hair measurement was exactly twenty-three months ago when he started ingesting lead particulates in huge quantities. This man was racked with pain, colicky, diarrhea, weakness, seizures, and extreme brain damage."

I threw out a question: "Could Sam have lived much longer?"

Doctor Brithen answered with a no and then drew within himself. "Oh, Chief Feather, you must be the brother of the deceased, I'm so sorry to have upset you."

"No, you have relieved the tension in my life. It is I that should thank you."

We started to adjourn the meeting, and General Lance threw out another question completely unrelated to the subject. "Doctor, are you employed at the present time?"

"Ah, oh well, no sir, the funeral home where I do work occasionally is about to go under, and I don't get much work anymore. Just a few embalming jobs a year is all."

"Would you like to go have some lunch with us? We're going to the mess hall, and I bet you've never eaten a good meal off of the United States government before."

"Ah, oh well, no sir, I haven't." We locked up and took the hungry doctor to lunch and wouldn't you know it, something on toast was the entrée of the day. The general and I stumbled through the line, but Doctor Brithen stopped at each pan and helped himself to a huge serving of everything. How he got around all that food was a mystery, but the dessert table lost several helpings too.

We convened our meeting in General Lance's office. He got his card, address, and tried to get his telephone number when it struck us that he didn't have a telephone. Then General Lance told Doctor Brithen to go get his time card. He wanted to see it. As he shuffled down the hall, we both agreed we needed this card in our deck. True to form, the little ole man showed up with star-struck eyes and presented his card to the general.

"Doctor Brithen, you have spent the better part of three days on this base, and you don't have enough time on this card. I want you to fill out the days completely and not cheat yourself out of pay. Now, we are working on a very delicate piece of land on the Cimarron River. I am going to swear you to silence from saying anything about this Sam Feather. I say again, don't talk to anyone about this, do you understand?"

"Oh, oh yes sir, my lips are sealed. You won't have to worry about me."

"Okay, Doctor, take your time card down to the paymaster, and he will pay you in cash for your time." I had to look the other way. I thought the kindly little man was going to kiss the general's ring!

As the kindly doctor exited the office, I about busted up. "Chief Feather, don't you say a word about this to anybody. I would never live this down. I want you to take over the Cimarron expedition. I think the Rangers have just about found all the F109-HE projectiles and are defusing the computer. To catch you up to speed, your brother Sam Feather just twenty-two months ago purchased eight rounds of 155-millimeter fragmentation bombs from the international black market. How they got them into Oklahoma, we can only guess. We suspect a covert operation boated them up the Cimarron River and was offloaded on your land. We have accounted for seven in the caves and are looking for the last one.

"Where Sam came up with the money for the bombs, we don't have a clue. We thought you might be able to figure this puzzle out. Total expenditure by Sam had to be close to sixteen thousand dollars, plus freight. Sam mustered out of the service two years ago with something less than two thousand dollars, and nobody has seen hide nor hair of him except an occasional glimpse on the river. We have traced his movements on the river where he had a track hoe on the sandbar and installed a pipe from Yonder Rock to the pit, dug a large deep hole in the sandbar, and filled the pit with quicksand. We figure all he had to do was go sit on Yonder Rock and the pit would fill in less than ten minutes. I want *you* to take over and complete the task you started. Do you have any questions?"

"When can Mr. Brithen start to work for me?"

"I will start a background check tonight, and it should be completed by the time you are ready to start moving equipment to the site."

"Okay, General, I should know something definite tomorrow. Before I go, let's go into your inner office. I have something to show you." I got out my lead marbles and set them on a slanted drafting table and let one go. It wobbled its way to the general, who caught it and looked at it closely. We tried each one, and they all wobbled the same.

General Lance asked quietly, "Why?"

"It's my turn to swear you to secrecy." All the general would do was squint my direction. "General, you remember when we went down on the river at night and I found the laser light?"

"Yes, we were in the cave under Yonder Rock. What has that got to do with these lead marbles?"

I produced my last lead marble that had been cut into and showed him the gold that was buried inside. "All of these lead marbles are gold covered with lead. At today's price, there is over twenty-five hundred dollars of pure gold in each ingot. I don't have a clue how many marbles are in that cave. I intend to pick up all the lead and weigh it against the marbles that I have, and I think we can find out how much was in the cave at one time.

"Now, General Norman Lance, all of these lead marbles are sized to go through a fifty-caliber Kentucky Long Rifle. Let me ask you a question. How many buffalo have been shot with lead-lined gold balls and nobody ever questioned the results?" All we could do was shrug our shoulders. Whoever cast these gold-lead balls was a gunsmith; they were within tolerances to go through a modern black power gun.

General Lance was not one to be quiet very long. "You mean to tell me that cave was a gunsmith's work shop?"

I countered with, "I don't have a clue what all this is about, but after discovering the magnitude of these marbles, the spirit circle, and Sam's death, I think we should double the guard on the section of land until such a time we can decipher this all out."

General Lance grabbed the phone and contacted security and put an all-out scramble to set up a dense parameter around that old Cimarron River and the section of land. I left him to his side of the scramble. I had a bed that was mine, and I didn't know when I would get back to it.

"Chief Feather, *Chief Feather,* wake up, Chief Feather!"

"Yes, yes, what do you want?"

"Chief Feather, General Lance wants you to report to his office immediately!" I could see the orderly was not going to be satisfied with a grunt. He wanted me fully awake. I got into my flight suit and boots and slogged myself out of the barracks into the office of the general. On the way, I did notice 0200 being the hour, *boy of all things!*

General didn't look as good as me, and we forgot to salute, *Well, whoop-de-doo.* "Ah, Chief Feather, there is a problem down on the Cimarron River, and I want you to take a contingent of my rangers and find out the true circumstances of the matter."

"Who are the intruders?"

"That is what we must find out. The MP's noted a medium-sized Kodiak landing craft coming up the river. They fired warning shots, and the craft broke silence and went off up the river. I want to know who is trying to stir up trouble. You take your Black Hawk and an Apache; scan for heat signatures for at least fifty miles up river until we find them. Take all the rangers that show up ASAP."

I thought, *this is turning to be a full fledged war. Who will show up next?*

I ran to my ship and was met with eight rangers in their suits, all blacked out. My air jockey had my bird warmed up, and we hit air as soon as my rpms topped out. I silenced my Black Hawk, and we hit the river with full electronics on search scan and recorded nothing. Apache Three was following at a discrete distance as we approached the river bridge. We could see the MP's out in force. I settled down for a full-fledged search and remembered that the Cimarron River got real shallow on up river. Apache Three set down on the sandbar in sight of the old Radiker Bridge and blacked out the ship so anybody coming down river would not see it until it was too late.

I ran the Cimarron River almost to Guthrie, Oklahoma, and never saw a blip. This time, I slowed down and hovered between the banks of that ole Cimarron going down river. I saw an outline or two but nothing definitive. I heard Ap Three come back on the air with, "Lone One, we have contact with a floating craft about three-fourths of a mile out and closing."

I rose out of the riverbed and could see both crafts on my Forward Looking Infrared Radar scope. "Ap Three, I'm going to spotlight them, and you stand by in case I get return fire." I was a good half mile away and several hundred feet in the air when my scope spotted the telltale signs of human occupation. I turned on my ten-million-candle power light and almost instantly saw fire flashes from the Kodiak. Apache spoke with a small flash-bang rocket. I saw on my scope the occupants hurtling out into the river. I set down close by and let the rangers do their job. The flash bang had stunned the floaters in the water and left one dazed in the Kodiak, and the rangers had the four surprises of the night.

"Fox One, I need a secure bus to transport the crew and Kodiak landing craft back to Fort Sill. Inform General Lance that we will stand by until further notice."

"Affirmative, Lone One, stand by for General Lance." I thought, *There just might be a boat trailer waiting for this Kodiak.* "Ap Three, scan down river for at least fifty miles. There has got to be a trailer waiting to pick up that landing craft."

"Roger, Lone One." The Rangers had all four scruffs banded together back-to-back on a sandbar awaiting transportation as daylight broke. *Oh well, might as well find out what the MP's are having for breakfast.* I sat down on the south river bank and took a verbal report from Master Sergeant Edders. They couldn't add anything to the fray as General Lance came on the air. "Lone One?" I gave him a complete report, and he said that Dr. Brithen was cleared to come to the site and begin his examination.

"Fox One, I need two Mash units set up on the hill top one for Dr. Brithen and one to stand by. Fox One, we have at least two dozen men on duty at the present time. Send me a stocked field kitchen with capabilities of feeding fifty men for the duration. I'm sending you four detainees for interrogation and a Kodiak landing craft with all their gear aboard. I have an Apache equipped with hellfire rockets scanning down river for any trailer that will haul the Kodiak. Send me a field-secured bus in case we have any other incursions on this property. I need a field surveyor to define the parameters of all the Indian lands in the area. General Lance, I've got traffic from Ap Three."

"Okay, Chief Feather, I will start all this equipment headed your way. I switched channels and received a notice from Ap Three that it had made contact with the Kodiak's trailer about twenty miles downstream and was holding the subject at bay."

"Ap Three, stand by; my ETA will be in twelve minutes." I picked up three of my rangers and made air time to the Apache. Now imagine this: here was a multi-million dollar Apache, bristling with every known armament, holding two women at a boat dock, scared to death, trembling, crying, wailing, and up flew a Black Hawk complete with rangers. My rangers disembarked and set up a parameter around my ship, and I stepped out on the tarmac with my helmet and flight suit on. I thought they were going to pass out.

I've seen bad guys, good guys that would have slit your gullet open, big, little, old, young, women pregnant, people in all kinds of shape, but here was two potty, squatty women scared for their lives. I calmly took my helmet off, and they gasped their last breath at seeing a full-blood Cherokee Indian that just said "Hi." They both swooned on the boat dock. We stood there and watched all that flab stacked on top of each other. The rangers got some water, threw it on them, and all they could do was sob and sit up. This was more than we could stand. We smiled and kind of looked the other way, and I asked what they were doing on the boat dock. They both tried to talk at the same time and made a mess of that. "Ah, we just waitin' on Bubba!"

"And who is Bubba," I asked.

"Oh," both retorted, "he is our bub an' wess is spost to pick 'em up."

I asked simply, "Who is 'em?"

"Oh, Bubba took our husbands and poppa up river nite fishin.'.

I mulled this over and asked them their names. Nell and Pell came out as one. "Okay, girls, my name is

Chief Lone Feather of the United States Army, and if I'm right, you girls are twins."

"You bet." They spoke as one.

"And you are waiting on your twin husbands, Poppa and Bubba."

"Yes," as one. *Ah, I should have known that one too.*

"Nell and Pell, have you ever had coffee in a Black Hawk helicopter before?" They both shook their heads. *I should have known "no."*

"Okay, let's all get seated in the iron bird, and I will try to straighten this fiasco out." I left the crew to make coffee and seat Nell and Pell while I got on the horn and talked to the powers that be.

"Ap Three stand down we have the situation in hand. Let's all fly back to base camp, and we will see what the other group has to say."

"Fox One, we are returning to base camp to interrogate four men. I feel that a big mistake has been made on everybody's part. I will report post haste." I lifted off real smooth, and the girls' eyes were taking it all in. A short ten later, we were sitting on a sandbar up river from the four that were still tied together. The lone Kodiak sat bobbing the water, and I thought, *What a peaceful scene this could be if all this military gear had never been invented.* I left Nell and Pell with their sweet coffee and talked with my rangers and explained what I had found at the boat dock. We stepped down to the Kodiak and got the surprise of the day: there was several flathead catfish swimming around in the boat. I pondered this and spoke quietly. "You know, Sergeant, I have never seen terrorists fishing. Carrying a good mess of catfish in his boat, have you?"

"No sir, Chief Feather, I think you should talk with these country hicks. There is something awful wrong here."

"Yes, yes, Sergeant. Before I do, is there a big, hairy ape tied up there named Bubba?"

"Yes, sir, there is a set of twins and an older man."

"Have you searched the boat for small arms?"

"Yes, sir, and I didn't find any guns, but I did find a small can of round sinkers, and some kind of a signal blanket that they have been covering up with."

"Okay, Sergeant, let's see that blanket first." It was a homemade blanket that had all kinds of tin foil tied to it. The small can of sinkers was produced, and I know my jaw dropped. Fifty-caliber balls for a Kentucky Long Tom Gun, namely the ones we found in Yonder Rock.

I walked back to my Black Hawk and ordered four more cups of strong coffee. The rangers cut the bands off of the family, and we all sat down in the warm sand and shared the first cup of the day. The girls swarmed their husbands as we settled down to a good ole-fashioned chat. Here were two couples and a brother and their dad, out on a night of fishin' in the Cimarron River and had gotten caught by millions of dollars of military equipment and the goods in a can. I told them about me fishing this very water and catching fish not unlike the ones in the boat. I ventured on the subject of the sinkers, and Bubba spoke up and said they weren't no good, you couldn't tie a string on them any way you tried. He had just left them in the boat to throw at the turtles and snakes. I asked him if he had any more, and he replied, "Naw we bout out."

I asked them if they knew a Sam Feather. You should have seen the hate start to boil. Bubba, the spokesman, explained that Sam had hired them to deliver eight heavy boxes to that rock that was down on the south side of the river by the bridge. He had a truck come to the boat dock at Manford, load the boxes in their rubber boat, and they delivered them to that rock. "That's been two years now, and all we got was the say so to fish all along them rocks. We ain't seed hide or hair of him and he still owes us."

"Okay, Bubba, this story is too strange not to be the truth, but we would like to see your catch." I kept his lead marbles with the promise they would be returned at a future date.

I contacted General Lance and gave my report except the lead marbles. His only reaction was his recommendation to save that in my computer, and someday we would sort this all out. I put the rubber boat back on the course for the Mannford boat ramp.

We set up base camp, tents, field kitchen, and spare security buses. The MASH unit went up for Mr. Brithen, which he converted to a morgue, complete with cold rooms. The field kitchens cooked breakfast the first day with all the powdered eggs anybody could want. I think that Mr. Brithen was the first and last customer. A private company came with Porto Potties, and we were in business of unraveling the mystery of the bones, lead, dye, and spirit circle.

The ordnance people came and reported that they had found the last 155-shell and that they were going to disarm the remaining seven sometime that afternoon. The Ap Three crew and I wanted a landing pad, so the engineering squad from Fort Sill showed up with landing mats and tie downs. We had to block the road coming down to the river, and we set up a permanent guard pen and felt the area was secured.

General Lance called from Fort Sill and wanted to send me a new device for disarming projectiles out in the field. I advised the ordnance people, and they set up a staging area for disarming the 155-millimeter projectiles. I don't know what I expected, but the first demolition was a mess of white smoke. I wanted to hear the real results! It was not to be; the rest of the shells were old hat, each with tons of white smoke. To me, the results were a dud, but the ordnance people were satisfied.

First things first, the post sent us a company of privates complete with contamination suits and Scuba gear. They picked up every single speck of lead slag that had been blown up by the first 155-millimeter shell. The night detail looked with black lights and found another bucketful. This played out over three days, and our camp was abuzz with excitement. A large dump valve was found out in the grass and became an item on the found tables that nobody knew where it fit in the puzzle. After the cleanup crew left, a crime lab was set up and they began the impossible task of finding the secrets of Yonder Rock.

Apache Three crew was called back to Fort Sill, and I was left as commanding officer. A communication tent was manned twenty-four seven, and I received a call from Bubba inviting me to go on a midnight fishing expedition. I couldn't say no and met the hairy ape at Yonder Rock just before dark, in no less but his rubber boat and the twin brothers-in-law. I had called the MP's off for the night, and we slipped out in the current as silent as the water ran. A short ride upstream put us on the rocky side of the river. We stepped out into the tepid water, and my mind flashed back twenty-five years to when my grandfather, Wounded Nose, took me on my first hand fishing with his bare hands, and I got to carry the sack.

I held the boat, and Bubba and his two brothers-in-law started in the old ways of catching those flathead catfish. We didn't catch too much until one of the old males tried to swim over me. I about ran up on the bank, boat or no. Oh, did they laugh at the green horn getting spooked. The action picked up as we neared Yonder Rock, and Bubba dove down under the bank and brought up a catfish the size of my leg, flipped her in the boat, and stated, "Boys, there's a gooder one in that old cave, and I can't handle her by myself."

I reluctantly stated that I had done this before and to let me help. "Chief, are you sho' you want that catfish to get ahold a yo' arm?"

"Bubba, I've been bit by the best. Let me help you." Bubba and I let the twins put their feet on us and pushed us into a cave under Yonder Rock and held us there. I've been hit by shrapnel, bit by dogs, pushed in a mud hole by a water buffalo, and flown into a hailstorm of small arms fire. The feeling that went through my arm when that flathead catfish clamped all seventy-two pounds of its weight on my arm was the accumulation of all the pain I had ever experienced. Fear ripped through my body to the furthest point. Bubba had brought a rope with him, and he got it through the fish's gills and pulled me, the catfish, and the rope out of the cave and threw us in the rubber boat. I was gasping for breath. The men were all laughing at me in the bottom of the boat acting like a flathead catfish, and the MP's turned on a spotlight to see the sight.

We gave up fishing that night and took all the fish up to the mess tent to butcher and clean them. Fort Sill had sent me several cooks, and they had a small guy from Arkansas. He claimed the cleanup job and said for everybody to come back tomorrow at noon and we would have fresh-caught, fried catfish and hush puppies. I looked at Bubba, and he spoke to me quietly, "Chief thems boys have got jobs to take care of, but me and the girls could come take thays place ifn you thinks its okay."

I put my arm around his barrel shoulders and thanked him for takin' me a fishin' and said any time he wanted to come to just let me know and he would always be welcome. "And Bubba, be shore and bring Nell and Pell tomorrow so I can apologize to them."

"Sho thing, Chief."

Sometime up in the morning, the MP's admitted Bubba and his twin sisters, Nell and Pell. Bubba made the comment, "You people are sure cleanin' up the old place. Chief, I needs to talk to you when you gots time."

"Okay, Bubba, let's walk out to my helicopter, and we can talk."

"Chief, I wants to be completely honest wid you. I told you the tother night that I didn has any mo' of them marbles, but I found a nother small can and you can have the whole mess."

"Bubba, I want to completely honest with you, too. Have you talked with Nell and Pell?"

"Yes, Chief, I has, and I know that you are Sam's blood brother, but you are like Sam was two years ago."

"Okay, Bubba, this might hurt you some, but it's happened, and I want you to know the whole story. We have a coroner with us, and he found that Sam died of extreme lead poisoning. It all started twenty-two months ago, when Sam started acting crazy. He died just two days ago, and I'm here trying to find out what happened. Bubba, have you tried to melt any of those lead marbles?"

"Yes sir, I sho have, and they all have a brass center, and I can't do anything with that."

All I could do was shake my head and wonder if he had gotten too much. "Bubba, did you feel bad after breathing that smoke that came off of them?"

"Sick. I thought I was going to die. I must have coughed for a week with just one session with those lead marbles. In fact, Chief, pour out those marbles. The brass ones are in the bottom."

"Okay, I believe all that you have told me, but let's let the chemical experts tell us what is wrong with that lead. Now Bubba, I have to know—are there any more of these marbles in your pockets, boat, home, or anywhere; if there are, don't handle them too much. Put them in a can and bring to me. I will return all the marbles to you when we are done with this inquiry. Is that understood?"

"Aww, Chief, you don't have to go to that much trouble, theys no good, anyway."

"No, that is not the point. Sam Feather wanted you to have them, and that's that."

"Okay, Chief. I just heard that Arkie call chow time. You s'pose we should dive in?"

As we walked toward the mess tent I thought, *The Lord has made all kinds of peoples.*

ONE FEATHER

My father, Miner Feather, came up missing one day from one of his trips. Big'ear and his dogs came in and announced that they were here, but no Miner, or Trader Joe, as some people called him. My mother Nell about grieved herself away and didn't last too long. An aboveground stand held her body until picked clean, and we put her bones into a hide bag. My brothers and I hand dug a grave in the hillside and gave her a Christian burial. All we had was a sandstone slab to mark our cemetery, and that seemed to be the best way to remember the ancient in this foreign land.

We couldn't remember moving over from Walnut Grove, Georgia, so this old hillside had become our home. Father never did farm too much, but it seemed we always had plenty to eat. Wasn't too long after my folks were gone we discovered that we had to work for our food! Big'ear wasn't much for pulling a plow, so us three men got together and worked out a deal for a team of mules. Our sister, Wind Song, did the cooking, and we did the farming. If I remember this correctly, we got tired of all that work real quick! My two brothers left home, and my sister and I stayed on and tried to feed ourselves.

The clan of Feathers broke completely apart. The Cherokee tribe lost all contact with us, and you might say we were on our own. My sister and I knew that she had been found on the trail to Indian Territory and adopted by my parents, but we didn't know what tribe or region she was from. Of course, we were scared to go or do anything. All we had was each other, and the natural way was to be married and live as man and wife. I scoured the countryside and found a few elders that were willing to go into counsel and witness. We stepped across a bow and became married on September 20, 1865.

Our first boy was born two years later, and this started a string of boy children coming into our lives. As with the ole Indian ways, we named our boys the way they acted or looked. Wounded Nose fell and had a crooked nose the rest of his life; this became the norm for eleven more children. My two mules were working the land, and we grew enough staples to feed us and sell the rest at the trading post. Big'ear became my stud donkey, and I would buy large mares and had little mules coming on all the time. There weren't any families that lived around us, and we had open range over several sections of land. I soon got out of the farming business and did my mule thing at the trading post. I would take a young team to the post, and most of the time, I could trade or sell them to farmers.

We had a large, open plateau south of our mule farm, and the elders from the neighboring tribes came and asked if they could meet on this space. I readily agreed, and plans were made for powwows for all the Indians that would come in the fall. The Indian agency of the time had declared we had Sac and Fox property on the south side of the Cimarron River as long as the water flowed. On the north side, the land belonged to the Pawnee's that we never saw. One day while sitting on Yonder Rock, I noticed smoke coming from off the bluff across the river. Since we had never had any neighbors show themselves on the north side, I took my own little braves and looked them up. Here was a large family of white people living back in the trees so far you couldn't see them. I thought, *Wind Song and I have a lot of kids, but this family has more than we do.* We cantered up to their dugout and just stared. This upset the whole lot, and they immediately got all the kids in the house and stuck guns out the windows, door, around trees; it was time for *us* to be scared. A rather short man came out, and would you believe it, he had hair under his nose, wore pants and shirt with string-like things over his shoulders. He signed to me, "Step down and lets have some sweet coffee together." I was surprised. I couldn't get over this white man that could sign to this Indian. I thought, *I wonder if he speaks English.*

I drew myself as straight as I could on my mule and spoke soundly. "Let's speak English. It's much easier." It was his turn to look surprised; we smiled at each other and communications were established across the races. All ten of us slipped off of our mounts, and William H. Fritch and One Feather got acquainted that morning over—what else?—a pot of coffee. The Fritch and the Feather kids broke racial boundaries that morning, playing on their side of the Cimarron River. We parted company that day with the promise that they would come over and visit Wind Song and me with all their kids. This grew into an understanding about other people that we never had known.

We had our plans made to have a powwow, but no deer were left to be had for the celebration. I made another trip across and wanted to trade a mule for a cow with Mr. Fritch. He didn't have a cow to spare but did have a pig. We traded back and forth some, and I knew then the ole boy was a trader deluxe. We finally settled on two pigs for two yearlin' mule colts. Mr. Fritch said to come back with the kill party, and he would have the pigs caught up for us. I confided in him and told the story of the Indians who wanted to hunt, kill, and dress their own game and that we were going to have a powwow on our land. "Mr. Fritch, I have a whole family of little braves that want to come and take the pigs home across their ponies, just like in the olden days." He saw my thinking and told me to come over and help ourselves. "Mr. William H. Fritch, whenever you are ready for your mules, come over and you can pick them out yourself."

The big day arrived, and we had our ten young braves ready to kill and eat all the roast hog they could hold. William had all his family out to watch the day the Indians killed the hogs. I knew that the white people fed the hogs out of a trough, and we gathered around to see the fun. Our good little braves took careful aim with their bow and arrows and missed the whole herd. All it did was spook the hogs, and they promptly ran into the woods. All the Fritches fell out around the dugout and laughed us to tears. My braves turned tail and wanted to go home.

I was laughing with William, and he saved the day with, "Alice, come out here. Call your hogs; we need to get these young braves something to eat." This little sprite of a girl came with her feed bucket; William brought a nice lever action gun and told Alice to get to calling.

"Now One, you tell me which ones you want, and I'll get you two hogs big enough to feed all your clan." We were ready for her to show us how to call the hogs. All she did was start banging on the side of her bucket, and hogs came out from behind every tree on the bluff.

"William, I want the spotted ones." Ker-blam! The first hog went down. Ker-blam! and the Indians had their meat for the powwow.

"One Feather, how are you going to get the hogs across the river?"

"We learned to drag the hair off of our game, you just watch." Ropes came out, and the Indian's mules started dragging them toward the river. One waved to the Fritches that day from the river bluffs, and our powwow started that night.

Doctor Brithen

Decontamination of the lower cave started with Doctor Brithen suiting up his crew with Scot packs, full body cover, and a large fan to stir the air. Engineering put up light banks inside and outside of the cave with a large generator set up downwind, and they worked around the clock inside the caves. Everybody was exiled away from the work site. Even General Lance called several times a day for updates. The cooks outdid themselves in the field, and we ate like kings. All the mess sergeant had to do was request a shipment of supplies, and it was sent from Fort Sill post haste. I made several recons of the area for topographic prints that the map department converted into a very detailed account of the cave system. Fort Sill sent all the support: the equipment, personnel, and we were set up for the duration.

Doc and I had morning meetings with his staff over breakfast. He asked me for a list of all the people that had been in the caves, even General Lance. I gave him the list of demolition people that were still working on the live bombs, and Doc stopped all work until the bombs had been taken care of. Seems the bombs had sufficient heat to start a new contamination over the whole section of land that we were in.

I called General Lance from my Black Hawk over a secure line. "General Lance, Doctor Brithen wants to examine you ASAP for lead contamination. He seemed to be in a hurry."

"Lone One, this is a secure line, but are you sure there is no one close by you?"

"No, sir, there are people all over the place. Wait a few and I'll lift my copter to another location." I revved the turbines into action and flew down on the Cimarron River and could see scores of people on the north side gawking their heads off. "General Lance, I'm in a hover above the river. Go ahead."

"Chief Feather, the word is out about gold across the Cimarron. I don't know where the leak got out, but be very careful what you show the public. Now what is this about Doctor Brithen wanting to examine me for lead contamination?"

"Yes, sir, he is making a complete sweep of all peoples that might have come into contact with the lead slag, marbles, the kiln, 155-millimeter shells, anything that has come into contact with this project."

"That sounds like Doctor Brithen is doing his job. Bring him to the base—he can examine me, have chow, and we can get a mid inquiry report."

"Sir, I'm not sure that is a good idea. I feel that we have become exposed to lead dust and should not leave this field base."

"Yes, I can see where you could feel that. Stand by. I'll catch a ride, have the exam, and we'll hear our reports in the field."

"Yes sir, in the meantime, send me several Apaches to do exercises down in the riverbed .We have onlookers by the score, and I'm sure they would like to swarm across the Cimarron to see what they can see."

"Ah yes, I'm sure the Apaches needs air time. They will be down presently."

I found Mr. Brithen in his element, examining bones. I told him that General Lance was coming and to get his exam kit ready. "Okay, Chief, let's take a walk down to the river. I need to clear my head out."

We could hear the Apaches coming by this time and witnessed a pass that cleared the complete north bank of gawking civilians. The Apaches put on an air show just for Doctor Brithen, and he was much revived by the time General Lance showed up. As they shook hands, we entered the private realm of Doctor Brithen. "Please be seated. I wanted to show you both a quark that I have found in the upper chamber of the cave. But first things first; General, let me look at your teeth and gums." A big grin got that job done, and a cheek swab seemed to satisfy the doctor.

"Doc, you mean you brought me down here just for that?"

"No, no, the examination is not over. I need a sample of your hair. What part do you want to lose?"

"Doc, you take whatever you need."

The good doctor was not a barber, but he did butcher some of the general's locks and stowed them in an envelope. "Now, good General, I need you for the next thirty minutes. Let's get a facemask on, and I want to show you a skeleton that I am examining."

We got our facemasks, walked into another room, and there was a little child not four feet tall. I asked Doctor Brithen what was wrong with the child.

"This is not a child. This man is fully grown at just under 48 inches tall and at least a century old."

"That can't be. Indians don't live that long!"

"Chief, don't ever be surprised at what you find in the graveyards. Look at his joints. This man has walked until his feet, knees, and hips are completely worn out; his left kneecap is completely gone. His head is half the size it should be, his teeth are worn down to the bone but are still serviceable. He was right-handed, and his right elbow is fused. His left hand has been broken multiple times and healed back, his right fingers are deformed like he was holding on to something flat."

"What did this man die of?"

"I haven't tested the bones or hair yet, but my guess is extreme extended exposure to old age and lead! Gentlemen, this man was a lead miner all his life: lived, worked, slept close enough to lead to kill six men. On the other table are his work clothes, hat, and walking stick. Now, General, for the rest of your examination, I need to turn the lights out and shine this black light on both of you." We shone like Halloween spooks. The miner and his clothing had the same glow.

"General Lance and Chief Feather, for your information only, I have the same purple glow all over me. The gravesite and explosion area is contaminated with this dye. The dye itself is not harmful except in the presence of at least five hundred degrees Fahrenheit. When I examined Sam Feather, I found the same purple dye in his lungs, flesh, and hair.

"General Lance, we have got to find the source of the dye or there could be an epidemic from this exposure." We told the doctor about the purple dye on our equipment and what the doctors had done to eliminate it from the equipment.

"General, I will expedite my examination, but I don't think you have had enough contact to hurt you. I have a request that may seem odd to you, but I believe we should take DNA tests of all the skeletons involved. It may help us trace the contamination of lead. I can take the cheek swabs, but the test will have to be conducted under laboratory conditions that we don't have in the field." General Lance and I agreed with Doctor Brithen, and we set up a daily courier helicopter for any tests that needed to be done.

"Chief Feather, I need a night scan video with black light for at least twenty square miles of the Cimarron bend area. I have a notion that whoever had the tainted lead must have mined it fairly close," said Dr Brithen.

"Chief Lone Feather, while you're here, I need a cheek swab for a DNA test. You will be my first patient." I thought, *I hope I won't be on his flat slab for my last.* "Oh oh, boys, I think our snack is ready. Let's retire to the mess tent and partake of some remains." We could see the good doctor wasn't affected by his findings.

Lone Feather Senior

My father, Wounded Nose Feather, was a stickler for command. He got us boys up at four o'clock every morning to milk cows and feed and water all the mules, all before breakfast. Our days were filled with work, hoeing, plowing, making hay, planting. Oh, did I hate work. My hands were always rough with the chores of the day. We ate well enough, but that hard work sealed my mind to never farm for a living. I wanted to fish, hunt, and lie around under some ole shade tree, watching the wars go on and on.

I was too young to be in World War Two or Korea but longed for a chance to do anything else. My parents even made me go to school, ride that yellow bus, put on clean clothes every other day, and do my homework. Father had worked that section of land until he and Kildare, my mother, were worn completely out and both stooped shouldered. For what? If they thought they would give me that land as an inheritance, forget that. I even saw the land patent one day that showed my Great Grandfather Miner had settled on this Indian land in 1811. The generations were: Miner, One, Wounded Nose, and I'm sure my folks were going to want my name, Lone, on there too. I was not impressed with the idea that I would be tied to the land forever!

I would hurry and do my chores, swim over the Cimarron River, and go to my number one buddy Pat's house on the north side of the river. We would hunt and fish to our hearts content until I had to go home at night. I knew that I was going to get strapped, but what else was news? We had been in the same grade at Schlegal School, then on to Yale, Oklahoma, for our fourth grade year. Pat and I were in the minority but had run the Cimarron River banks, were play and work hardened when school started that fall of 1945. The second day of school, the city slickers tried to put the hurt on us, but all the kids from Schlegal School backed up to the Harding School wall, and did we frail the daylights out of them! Oh, we put the roust to those kids and ran them into the schoolhouse. Our blood ran hot that day, and we loved the rush. All we had to do was look mean, and city slickers would start to whine. I don't know how much the teachers taught us, but Pat and I were cemented together. If it hadn't been for that breed, I would have left school and never thought anything about it.

My little brother, Jim, was always in the way, told on me, or put up his sass; we would pin his ears back, but he always came back with that sassing smirk that set me off. I would pound him until my hands were sore, and he always came back for more. I tried, oh, I tried to get into that thing called schoolwork, but the lessons never stuck very long. I dropped out to never start again. Sad, bad, ignorant—that was the choice I made, and I determined myself to live it.

As soon as I turned eighteen, I was out of there to never go back to that farming life again. I enlisted in the Army and loved the challenge of boot camp; they taught me how to survive under the worst of conditions. When war broke out in Viet Nam, our company was first in line.

Life on a war front was the best rush a real man could experience. Hourly we were called on for another emergency. The bad guys were everywhere, and we lived on the very edge of excitement. The very first time I made a kill, I felt the Indian hot blood rush through my veins. Our companies were called the "Soldiers of the Winds from Oklahoma." The enemy could be from any of several countries. We lumped them all together and called them the bad guys. Our Sergeant Ames drilled into our thick heads that the only way to fight was together. Everything depended on each other, and never were we to face a fire fight one on one. Our backside had to be covered by the next company, and we were spaced out exactly right to protect the next company. Our Sergeant Ames must have known his stuff because we survived against tremendous odds. I have never thought about so many enemies in all my nineteen years as could come over the Mekong River. My Cimarron River in Oklahoma was but a creek compared to the size of the Mekong.

We heard about the Tet expansion, and all we could think was "bring them on." Sergeant Ames warned us; we retorted, "Soldiers of the Winds from Oklahoma." Our sleep was interrupted every minute—bombs were detonated around the clock, and screams a million strong penetrated our innermost thoughts.

Sergeant Ames, the old man of the company, had just turned twenty-four the night they struck. All we could visualize was victory by daylight. The bad guys came in waves all night long, screaming like banshees. Rocket fire burst like fireflies in the brush. We never knew if the bad guys were in front or behind us. We were supplied hourly with ammo and would almost run out before Supply Company brought new shell cans. The first time we knew we were surrounded, we heard cries from all around. The dead bodies stacked up all around our company and more came screeching through. My ammo was played out, and the only weapon used was bayonet hand-to-hand combat. I heard my last sound when a fragmentation round went through my helmet.

Screams, groans, cries of anguish, then Viet dialect in a stream. I woke up to all this, realized it was me doing the crying. My thumbs were wired behind my back, and I was trying to pull one of them off. I never have had pain like that in my nineteen years. Sergeant Ames was talking to us and told us that he had called for the B-52's to bomb our location as a bamboo bayonet sliced through his chest. I looked around; there were several of my buddies already hung in the trees with their arms flailing their last swing.

My turn came when a wire noose buried itself in my neck muscles. I was jerked off the ground. I was able to pull my thumb off and flail the air. I tried to loosen the embedded wire, and my fingernails went through my flesh. As the blood vessels exploded around the wire, I smiled to the bad guys and could hear the rolling thunder start their destruction. My last thoughts were, *Those bad guys will vaporize just like me in a Viet Nam stinking swamp.*

Night Stalker

"Chief Feather, we have a subject that is setting up surveillance on the other side of the river. They don't have any binoculars or listening equipment, only an old dog for company. Sometimes she comes at night and stays two or three hours and the same in the afternoon almost every day. We can't figure out if she is a threat or just curious. She never hides or tries to conceal her identity in any way. In fact, she has cut a trail around the north side of the river to a house that is five thousand meters away. We have night vision prints that show the exact trail, daylight face prints of her, the dog, and her house. We thought it might be some of your relatives."

I took one look and recognized Little Bird, Sam's wife; the rest of the pictures didn't make sense. "Run a security check on Little Bird Feather, and we'll see what's going on." The report showed her marriage to Sam, the divorce of 1958, and absolutely nothing could be found since that time.

I hid the next day and observed the subject with binoculars. Sure enough, Little Bird came and sat her three hours and left the same way she came. I had not seen her since Sam, and she had married in 1954, her Indian beauty shining as a young princess in white man's clothes. My heart stung at the thought of Little Bird being alone, not knowing the complete story of Sam. I let my thoughts wonder about my own life, not ever being married, what Little Bird was doing with her life, what we could do with ours. My mind slammed shut with that last thought. I was married to the armed services for ever!

I let time play out and watched Little Bird leave; I'm sure both of us felt the pronging of incompleteness.

LITTLE BIRD

Sixteen was my magical year, my dream come true. I made plans of spending my complete lifetime with that scamp Sam Feather. Oh, I knew we should have finished school, went on to college, gotten an education, but we were so in love and on a whim we married in the spring of 1954. Sam was the best of husbands; we loved each other with passion known only to Indians. We could run the banks of the Cimarron River with the lusts of panting deer and sleep day or night with the abandonment of the animals. Our lives were united "down on the ole home place" with the death of Lone, his father. A section of land that carried the Land Patent of 1812 was deeded to Sam, the eldest of two.

Sam and Lone Jr., his twin brother, were called into the army and took their boot camp together. Lone took helicopter training; Sam took advanced training with the seals. This put both of them in Kuwait and Iraq. A long, bitter struggle seared Sam's mind, and he came

129

home a changed man. Oh, he still loved me, but his love was mixed with violent outbursts of rage. I carried bruise marks for as long as I could and divorced him two years ago. We were childless and that put me out of his life with only a small settlement. I tried and succeeded to hide from his life. As I healed up, I decided to never bother him again.

My Great Aunt Kildare took me in. I guessed we needed help, and a bond was made that hid me from all the strife. Aunt Kildare and I heard the first helicopter sounds echoing down the Cimarron River. Auntie spoke quietly in the night, "Little Bird, what is that 'whop whop' sound on the river wind?"

"Auntie, I think it's a large helicopter. I can't think what is going on. I will take Dog (yes, that was his name), and track that sound in the morning."

My old Auntie could hardly walk anymore, but her hearing was as acute as ever. I had moved in with her when my divorce was final, and we took care of each other. I took Dog with me and hiked around Keller rocks on the Cimarron River. I heard the helicopter leave and knew the hike was useless for the day. My return home was through the warm river waters; I let my mind wonder how many times I slithered on my stomach through the red mud. *Oh! Little Bird, those times are over for now!*

"Yes Auntie, that was a helicopter on the sandbar by the old home place. I can't think why any one would want to visit that place. It's so overgrown with brush you can hardly see Yonder Rock."

"Oh Little Bird, let's not think about those days anymore. We can't help Sam." I dismissed the thoughts, but in the back of my mind I was wishing I knew what was going on.

The very next afternoon was when we heard the explosion. Asleep, dreaming, Dog was barking at the winds, all the water fowl were flying crazy, and I was up running around in circles trying to get my mind to settle down. Dog and I hiked down river and saw the remains of Yonder Rock. I thought, *Good, somebody has blown that ole hillside to smithereens. Sam spent countless hours messing around the hill. I hope he was inside!* I discovered that day that hate remained among my innermost feelings.

"Oh Auntie, I still hate Sam for what he did to me. How can I forgive him?" All Auntie did was hold my sobbing shoulders and rock back and forth. I told her the complete story of when Sam had gotten so mean, our senseless fights, beatings that left my mind scarred, the days that he would spend inside Yonder Rock and come out a raging maniac.

"Why, Auntie?"

Aunt Kildare spoke so kindly. "Little Bird, we don't know all that the Lord has in store for us, why we have to go through these hard times. We can only stay under his will and all this will pass in time. Time has a way of healing that we don't understand. Now, Little Bird, I want you to go back and face your worst fears. I would go back, but my knees will not stand the walk, but I want you to tell me everything that has happened on Yonder Rock."

I did as Auntie said and watched the lights at night, sometimes at day, made myself a path for Dog and I, and became one with the river. I don't know how long this surveillance lasted, but I didn't learn one thing from watching across the river. I had to get closer, see people up close, and make the biggest mistake of the age.

The very next night, Dog and I crept out on the sandbar and set up my surveillance next to the water. This helped me hear more, but the high bank kept me from seeing anything. I thought, *I'll creep up on the south bank and there I can see what is going on.* Dog was scared of running water, but I was a water dog to the core. The only problem I had was I got water in my boots and they sloshed too much. I made the high bank and was surrounded with men in black! They strapped my thumbs behind my back, threw a net over my head, and led me unceremoniously to the guard shack. A quick pat down with a female guard produced my dog leash and nothing else. A M/SGT led me into an interrogation tent. I was put on a stool, and my restraints were removed. Armed guards were at attention, and the questions started.

M/sgt Pattie Anderson introduced herself and asked what my name was. I didn't see any need to lie, and I very timidly told her "Little Bird Feather."

"Okay, Little Bird, what are you doing spying on an United States investigation?"

I didn't have a clue what she was talking about. All I knew to say was: "I was watching the ole home place of the Feather Clan."

"Very well, M/sgt Anderson, I will take over now," came a voice that I had heard before. I looked and about fainted. There stood *Sam,* my ex-husband, in full camo fatigues. I had to restrain myself; it was as if Sam had changed back to his own self and was all right.

"Little Bird, it's good to see you again. It's been a long time," this familiar voice came to me. I just couldn't believe my eyes and ears when the voice introduced himself. "Little Bird, I'm Lone Feather, Sam's brother." That's it. I lost my composure and cried my eyes out.

"M/sgt Anderson, have the guards stand down, but I want you to stand by with a recorder. I want to talk with Little Bird about what is going on."

"Chief Feather, this is an official investigation. Be advised that Little Bird is not cleared through security at this time."

"Yes, bring the recorder, and we will have a tape of all that is said."

"Yes sir, one moment please." With tape recorder in place and official introductions recorded, Lone told me the status of the Feather Family.

"Little Bird, you were the wife of my brother Sam and were divorced some months ago, is that correct?"

"Yes, I can't remember just how long, but my heart still hurts sometimes."

"Yes, mine does too, but we must get on with life as dealt out to us. You have been observed in surveillance of the Feather property. Are you in these pictures?" I looked at myself in full view of the camera and felt like a dummy.

"Yes, that is me. What can I do?"

"This is a night view of the pathway that you carved out of the brush, is it not?"

"Yes, I'm guilty and I'm sorry. What can I do?"

Another picture was produced, and Lone asked me was this his great aunt Kildare? It was Lone's turn to tear up when I said yes, it was.

"How old is Aunt Kildare?"

"Lone, we don't know. All the records are gone, and she can't remember."

"All the questions that you have been asked are confidential information at this time. You will have to live with that answer until this investigation is complete. Can you live with that?"

"Yes sir, Chief Feather, I will tell Auntie nothing."

"Now, Little Bird, you don't have to call me Chief. Only the enlisted men do that. I want you to go home and not tell anybody anything about what you have seen here tonight. Is that clear?"

"Your men threw a net over my head; all that I could see was a few lights and you with Pattie Anderson."

"Very good. Now, M/SGT Anderson, call your guard, bind Little Bird and throw that net over her head, and escort her across to Dog. I'm sure he will be glad to see her."

I thought, *That Chief knows all about me!* I went home that night the long way so I could think my way around all the questions of Auntie.

Doctors

There was seldom a briefing session each morning that Doctor Brithin didn't have a question, request, statement, or comment. This morning's request was for an archaeologist. I asked why. As the doctor started in, I thought, *There goes more money and time.*

"No, Chief Feather, you've hired me to track this lead contamination. My specialty is bones, not rocks. Let's call General Lance in, and I'll walk through what I know at the present time." *Yeah, I bet he wants to know about a few rocks,* I thought. "Mr. Chief, *there* is a lot to be learned from a good rock hound."

Good grief, I thought, *Doc can read minds, too!*

"Yes, the skull can say a lot, too," he retorted.

"Doctor Brithen, I will send a request for a good archaeologist as soon as the channel is open this morning."

"Mr. Chief, I didn't say a good archaeologist, I specifically said archaeologist."

"Okay, whom do you want *specifically?*"

"Oh, I'm glad you asked. I want a man named George Askin from the alcohol rehabilitation center in Shawnee. We are alumni of the Oklahoma University class of 44". You will need to go to Shawnee to pick him up, as he doesn't drive any more. Oh, and Mr. Chief, don't let him stop anywhere and imbibe at the local taverns."

"Okay, I will call General Lance and start clearance checks so he can come in on this inquiry. Is there anything else I can get for you this morning?"

"Oh, why yes, there is. Have twelve dozen small laundry baskets delivered. We are going to need them to display bones, ah, ASAP as you would say.

"I started to think and stopped."

"Yes, Mr. Chief, you started to think."

Yes Doctor Brithen, I started, stopped, and realized you were ahead of me. I will order your laundry baskets ASAP!

That young Mr. Chief sure talks in riddles, I wonder what a sap means?

I relied on my Black Hawk for a secured channel and got General Lance on the first try. "Doctor Brithen has called an updated session with you to view the current progress. What is your schedule?"

"Chief, the map department has a presentation that will surprise all of us. Let's meet on site for noon chow, start the briefing, and go until we're through."

"Okay, I will relay a message to Doc, and we'll be ready at that time."

I looked up Doctor Brithen onsite. As I suited up, he very quietly took me to the middle chamber and told me they had found a very delicate map, journal, and writing quill. The very bright lights showed us the ceiling with all kinds of hieroglyphics. One of the shelves held what looked like a map, book, and a quill. A black light showed us the complete cave was contaminated with purple dye, lead slag, and most of all, there was a container of round lead balls. "Chief Feather, this looks like the scribing room to me. I have blocked off all traffic until we can get an archaeologist to date these writings and make a grid of where everything is located. All this will have to be done with the utmost care for fear of contamination. In the meantime, let's back out of here and get into clothes that are much more comfortable. I need fresh air."

I took the good doctor to the Cimarron River bank, and we visited until the morning briefing was scheduled. We gathered in the conference room, and I was notified that General Lance would be a few minutes late, that he was airborne as we spoke. The cook got us coffee, and we propped our feet up and started telling lies when I heard the copters from Fort Sill arrive. I straightened my tie, wiped my boots, and was standing at attention on time.

General Lance showed up in camo fatigues and gave the nod to speak privately with me. "We are on field patrol while on this inquiry. I know you don't dress like that while I'm not here; go make me feel at home and change into your fatigues." I turned that certain red around the collar and left to make myself a little more comfortable.

As I rejoined the briefing, in strolled a little ole man, spiffily dressed with his striped pants and loafers. I thought, *This has to be Doctor George Askin.* The doctors put on a good-old-time, get-acquainted show. All the brass had to do was look on and smile. These two were ole cronies from the class of 44' at OU and were working on the same project again. Needless to say, the briefing didn't get much said, chow was called, and guess who was first in line? Yep, those two were as hungry as bears, and we let them have the first chance at the entrée of the day.

We got down to business after the chow line emptied and Doctor Askin was suited with a doctor's cape. The map department brought the typographic layout of the complete section of the Feathers' land. Doctor Brithen spoke of the discovery of several bone bags in the upper chambers. Pictures of the skeleton confirmed his warning about contamination of lead dust, purple dye, and the need to not handle any artifacts until Doctor Askin could make categories of the cave sites. Doctor Brithen's report of the graveyard covered its sandstone slabs. His preliminary was that the graves weren't anything new; in fact, they ranged in age from 1850 to the present time. One abnormality turned up a complete donkey skeleton. Doctor Brithen didn't think the donkey was of any relation to any of the graveyard occupants.

Doctor Askin gave his preliminary view of the maps of the area and asked what were in the other graves up on the hill. All we could do was wonder with him. He called for an overhead screen and showed the ripples in the ground that indicated to him that the whole hillside had several mass graves. We didn't wonder any more why Doctor Brithen wanted the best there was. The general briefing broke up, and the meeting with the brass started with contamination suits and Scott Packs. The doctors lead the procession, and we started in the lower chamber. Doctor Brithen explained what each chamber was used for, lead slag that was taken out, weighed, and stored for future examination. How much contamination was produced when Yonder Rock exploded with a 155-millimeter projectile? Dr. Askin merely asked a question now and then and rubbed his beard. As we were ready to exit into the middle chamber, Doctor Askin asserted that the painted hieroglyphics on the back wall were quite old. He was asked how old they were and reserved that opinion until further carbon-dating tests could be conducted.

The entrance into the middle chamber showed more hieroglyphics, and Doctor Askin got excited. His opinion at this time was that they were well over fifteen hundred years old. Doctor Brithen showed the edges of the map, journal, writing quill, and the intention to grid the complete cave. Doctor Askin asked if we had taken any bone bags out of the upper cave. Again, we were speechless; we hadn't taken any.

Doctor George pointed out the mud layers under the rocks above the shelves. "Men, this can only mean one thing: this is the start of a whole cavern of spaces. If I'm not mistaken, we will find hundreds of hide bone sacks in the upper spaces." A black light showed the contamination of the entire middle cave. We could hear someone laughing, and it turned out to be Doctor Askin.

"This purple dye is the result of rainwater and oak leaves soaked in lead ore. Yes, it looks bad, but even if you heat it to the melting point of lead, it will not hurt the tissues of the body. It will stain them the purest purple and will outlast any washing powder you can use. Chief Feather, have someone bring some Cimarron River water to me."

I called for a bucket of river water, and it was soon produced. "Now, gentlemen, observe," said Doctor Askin as he threw the warm water on a side wall. The black light showed a complete cleanup of purple powder, and the color of the rock shone through. "Gentlemen, don't blame Doctor Brithen for this mistake; this trick has been used for millennia by the shaman of old. The salt in the river water reacts with the oak tannin solution, and the contamination will turn back to its original color immediately. Now, gentlemen, the act of melting lead will produce a vapor that is a very strong hazard to your lungs. Doctor Brithen, what is the hazard to bone?"

Doctor Brithen adjusted his glasses and responded, "Lead salts will impregnate the bones and will create brain, nerve, red blood cell, and digestive damage. The small skeleton that is displayed in the exam room is the result of lead poisoning. We don't know who this skeleton belongs to, but he was in constant contact with lead all his life and lived to be a very old man. That is called chronic poisoning. The Sam Feather body was a case of acute poisoning. He ingested large amounts of lead over a short period of time; the consequence was death. We have on display the very kiln that was used by Sam in the act of smelting these vast amounts of lead. He must have breathed in the vapor for months on end."

"Doctors, what are the results of the lead marbles that have been found?" asked General Lance.

The doctors looked at each other. "Nothing had been tested at this time." Doctor Brithen said," We have seen the marbles, but they have been gathered by Mr. Feather."

"Okay," General Lance spoke, "if any more marbles are discovered, turn them in to Chief Feather. We have determined that they were all cast to be shot through a fifty-caliber Kentucky Long Tom Gun. The gunsmith that cast them knew his business. Gentlemen, if there are not any more questions, I want to thank Doctor Brithen and Doctor Atkin for their expertise. Chief Feather, do you have any thing to add to this inquiry?"

I shook my head no.

"Doctor Askin, continue with the grid of the center chamber. We want to test the cave system for acoustics when you are done. Gentlemen, this briefing is over for the time being."

GREAT AUNT KILDARE FEATHER

Wounded Nose Feather was a hard man: hard on himself, kids, animals, people. Most of all, he was my husband. His name was on the land patent struck in 1811 by Grandfather Miner Feather from Walnut Grove, Georgia. The United States government had disposed of all the Indians from the southern states and relocated them to Indian Territory, which became the home of countless Indian tribes. Our section of land on the south side of the Cimarron River was the center of our lives. We farmed the land, raised mules, sold what we could to get along—and that was tough at times. Wounded Nose had never gone to school; he was determined to put our boys completely through.

　　Lone and Jim were the exact opposite of each other. Yes, we made them go to school. Lone couldn't seem to get the hang of education, but Jim was an honor student. If we wanted something done, Lone was the best, but Jim was the most level-headed. Lone, the restless one, joined up with the men of the winds, as he always said, "for the rush." Viet Nam swallowed men like water, and my Lone became one with the swamps. We never recovered his remains or ever knew where he rotted apart. That was the hardest part of my life, not knowing anything.

Jim was so passive; he missed his brother, disappeared in the United States, and I never knew where he went. Wounded Nose left me to be with his ancients, and we buried him in the family plot on this section of land. I couldn't stand living this close to my husband's body and moved around the river bend to live out my days on Indian land by myself. This little sprite called Little Bird Feather came to check on me one day, and all I can say is that she stayed on. We learned to lean on each other, and I could see that I was nearing the last of my days when the ruckus started on the old home place.

Little Bird came in from the night, and I felt that something was wrong. She didn't say a word, went to bed, and I could tell she wasn't asleep. I smelled something wet and discovered her wet boots on the back steps. I couldn't see much, but the smell reminded me of the river mud. I felt the boots and sure enough, there was red mud all over and inside too. I went in and said to her, "Little Bird, is everything okay?"

"Yes, Aunt Kildare, I'm tired and want to lie about and collect my thoughts."

"Little Bird, why are your boots full of wet mud?"

"Oh Auntie, it is something that I can't talk about just now. Just give me some time, space, and I'm sure it will all come to a head."

"Yes, time has a way of healing that I can't explain. Are you sure you are okay?"

"Yes, Auntie, I'm fine. Maybe we can talk about it in the morning."

"Dear, yes, we will have something to talk about tomorrow."

I sent word with Little Bird to have Lone come visit me, I knew he was in the military but had never met him. Our family had gotten torn apart with that rascal Sam, Little Bird was lucky to have got out when she could. We nurtured each other to health as good as we could. I will never understand how any man can beat the living daylights out of his mate. Bird as I called her came to me completely broken apart and would hardly leave her bed much less go outside for months on end. As Lone drove up in the yard with Bird I said a prayer that we could get all this craziness behind us.

"Lone it's so good to meet you, come let me lay my hand on your face maybe I can see something that I remember." Lone came to my rocking chair and knelt so gently, I immediately could see the family resemblance and couldn't help but see a lot of Sam in that strong brown Indian. Those twins had so much to share but they tell me Sam is dead and only Lone to carry the family name.

"Lone I have a story that needs to be passed to you from Miner Feather. I want you two to go upstairs and bring the wooden box of story hides, all of Miner's tools and anything else you want to know about."

Those two tripped up the stairs and only stayed a minute, as they came back Lone made a strange request. "Aunt Kildare we found the boxes of hides and tools but I want you to tell me about them before we move them." Lone had brought a recorder, and as he set it beside me, I asked Bird to bring me some water and we would get on with the telling.

"Years ago, when One Feather and his wife, Wind Song, were married, that's your great-grandfather and great-grandmother, they lived in this very house. Miner Feather was a traveling peddler to all the Indian tribes that lived along the Cimarron River. I never saw Miner Feather, but the tribes called him Trader Joe. Where he got that nickname, we never knew. He had a donkey named Big'ear that pulled a small wagon and always some old dogs. His trading brought corn, beans, trinkets, jerky, and sometimes flour or cornmeal in small sacks to the splintered clans. Miner would trade anything for anything just so you got the best of the deal. They told me that Great-Grandfather would laugh each time somebody got the best of the trade. I suppose those boxes of Miner's tools were left upstairs when he was traveling all over, and he thought he would pick them up sometime on his way through, I don't know. What all is there I can't remember. I remember playing with the marbles when I was a little girl and Momma getting so mad when she found me chewing on them. In fact, if you look in that long box, those teeth marks on the lead marbles are mine."

"Aunt Kildare, was Miner real short?"

"Lone, now remember I never saw him, but my Poppa said he could walk under your belt line with his big ole floppy hat on. His head was half again bigger than it should have been for anybody that small. He disappeared in 1863 and left the land, donkey, two dogs, and the small wagon for One and Wind Song to farm that section of land. They about starved out because the land had never been broken out. It seemed that Miner, his wife Nell, and the three boys had never farmed or did anything except make a small garden. Lone Feather Senior inherited the farm; the rest of his family disappeared in the neighboring tribes and were never found. One Feather and his wife stayed on that section for decades until Wounded Nose and I buried them in the family plots. I suppose you know where the graveyard is?"

"Yes, Aunt Kildare, I know. I need to get back to the camp and hold everything together. Is it all right if I bring one of my assistants back tomorrow? I would like for him to see the upstairs just like it is."

"Oh yes, Lone, please do whatever you want. You are the rightful heir to all this land; me and Little Bird are just squatters. Come and go as you please."

I saw that Auntie was getting tired and needed a nap. I turned to Little Bird. "Let's take a trip up river and check on the boundaries of this side of the river."

The Humvee proved much easier to get around in, and we let the wind blow across our faces. As the miles passed, we grew weary of the sounds and just stopped in the shallow water, savoring the moment. Little Bird and I sat and looked at each other, not saying a word.

"Lone, when I saw you the other night, it was as if Sam had been healed of his craziness, and I was to be whole again. That turned out to be a big disappointment on my part; I wanted to blame you for killing my husband. I wanted to hate you for destroying my life. I wanted you destroyed. As reason prevailed, I saw that you were a victim, the very same as I."

The arrival back at Aunt Kildare's house was heralded by Dog out in the yard. We bounded out of the Humvee, and Little Bird scolded her dog. "You silly dog, we're home, shut your—oh my word, Lone, look at Auntie!" The rocker's arms had cradled her frail body as she eased backward; the wide-open eyes and mouth showed volumes that we didn't want to see. A hand had fallen open in her lap; wisps of grey hair blew softly across her face without a hand to tuck it over an ear. The soft wind had caught up Great Aunt Kildare Feather's breath, to never come again this way. Little Bird and I looked at the precious body that would never move again under its own power.

Later Little Bird and I pondered if we should have a public funeral, a private service, or an aboveground presentation so the birds of the air could pick the bones clean. The answer came by Doctor Brithen. "Mr. Lone and Little Bird, this body is full-blood Indian; we are on Indian land that has been owned by the Feather family for two hundred years. You can make any decision that you want to; you are not bound by any laws of the land."

We made the decision at that point to have our own private service and bury her in our own graveyard by her ancients. My air jockey, Little Bird, a couple of the men from Fort Sill that were Indian, and I hand-dug her grave. We gathered around and said our goodbyes, wrapped Great Aunt Kildare's body in her best shawls and a hide rug, threw on the last of the dirt, covered the site with a large sandstone slab, and went on our way.

A lot can be said, but Auntie had fulfilled the life she wanted. Nothing else need to be said.

Reports

General Lance flew in unannounced with his arms full of reports. "Chief Feather, we need a good long briefing with the doctors. They have made an outstanding discovery, and you are the main subject. They may have a bearing on where we should go with the inquiry."

This does not sound good, but here we are, and I can't run now.

"We wanted you to hear this from us first, and then we will make plans. Chief Feather, you know the progress of the spirit circle?"

"Yes sir, we are waiting on Doctor Askin to clear the upper chamber so we can run some acoustics tests."

"Yes, that is right, and Doctor Askin, what are your findings?"

"I have documented all the hieroglyphics, moved the map, journal, and quill pen into the examination rooms, opened the entrance to another upper room, and stopped my work because of what I found. Gentlemen, I think we have found the secret of the spirit circle, the upper graveyards, and the complete cave system acoustics. I propose that we move our meeting into the upper chamber to examine the evidence. If you don't mind, let's all put on masks and coats to preserve the artifacts."

I couldn't get it out of my head that something was amiss but had to go along with the briefing. It was as Doctor Askin had said—all the artifacts were removed and the purple had been decontaminated with vaporized salt. The rocks had been removed from the upper entrance and lights installed to show hundreds of hide bone sacks. "There is no lead contamination in the recently discovered grave chambers. We stopped work because we didn't want to disturb the bone sacks. It is my estimation that these bones are at least two thousand years old and are in very poor condition," said Doctor Brithen.

"Gentlemen, place the spirit circle in the newly opened grave chambers." We began to hear outside noises, birds chirping, wind sounds.

Doctor Brithen took the spirit circle down, the noise stopped; he put it back, and we could hear the noises again. "Doctor Askin, you take over now. I will go outside to the spirit hole, and we will demonstrate more of the spirit's capabilities."

Doctor Askin explained the spirit hole was a group of crystalline rock on the surface of the ground over the upper chamber. We heard Doctor Brithen walking, and soon he was talking to the ground like he was talking to us. Doctor Askin told us that Doctor Brithen could not hear us. Sounds were only conducted one way. "General Lance and Chief Feather, this is an anomaly that defies my understanding of crystalline composition. In simple words, gentlemen, this is not supposed to happen in nature."

Doctor Brithen's voice came through the chambers, "Gentlemen, let's gather in the examination room, and we will continue the briefing."

We gathered back in the exam room and continued with the reports from the map department. Doctor Askin began with the night scopes films taken with the black lights. The overhead screen showed us the section of land that belonged to the Feather family, the Cimarron River sparkling like fireflies at night. "General Lance and Chief Feather, these specks are lead slag and dye that glow in black light."

"If you trace these lines, they are old trails that have long been grown over and no longer can be traced except with black light. These films cover a twenty-square-mile area, and the specks are the telltale sign that someone has scatted the slag to get it out from under Yonder Rock. We have determined that Yonder Rock was the central melting pot for all the lead. Whoever this was must have worked for over fifty years spreading this slag. I have done a lot of research on lead mines in the southeast portion of Oklahoma, and this is not the same composition of this lead. I expanded my research to all the states and have located a specific mine east of Atlanta, Georgia, that matches its description."

"Chief Feathers, the rest of the briefing will apply to your family. Do you know where your great-great-grandfather came from?"

"Negative, Doctor Askin, we have the original land patent filed by Miner Feather in 1811, his signature, and the following generations that have owned this section of land. I have the current transactions where I have control of this property."

"Do you have this patent with you?"

"'Negative, all those papers are in General Lance's safe in Fort Sill."

Doctor Askin turned to General Lance. "Do you have those papers with you?"

"Yes, they are all in this locked case."

"Gentlemen, please excuse Doctor Brithin and me for a few minutes while we examine the documents." I thought, *Now what can these doctors dig out of all those ole papers?* We could see the doctors pouring over the signatures and making their "yes, that looks okay, let's present our findings."

Doctor Brithen called the briefing back together. "General Lance, is seems we are about to solve the mystery of Yonder Rock. We want to present the complete Feather clan from 1810 to 2008. Lone Feather Junior, we are sorry that we can't produce the skeleton of your father. His remains were never recovered from the Mekong Delta, Viet Nam. Orderlies, please bring in gurneys numbers two and three."

Both skeletons were trundled into sight, and it was quite evident Wounded Nose was first. Doctor Brithen had us note the general worn condition of the joints, the stooped shoulders, and flat feet. This Indian was a farmer all his life. One Feather was next. He had the smaller skeleton of a hunter-gatherer, his joints were not as worn, and lived a comfortable life. "All of these skeletons match the DNA of Chief Feather. The last skeleton you have already seen, but we did not recognize him at that time. Gentlemen, I want you to become well acquainted with the oldest skeleton to date that we have found. Chief Lone Feather Jr., this is your great-great grandfather Miner Feather. All three-foot-eleven of a lead miner all his life, I estimate this skeleton to be 104 years old. We have no records of where he came from, only the lead in this cave matches lead taken from a mine in Walnut Grove, Georgia. We have found in the cave that you call Yonder Rock a complete set of gun projectile tools with bullet casting blocks all marked with MF. There is no doubt that these tools were the property of Miner Feather. He was not only a miner but a maker of rifle balls too. The measurements that we have made match the bullet casting blocks in use today for all fifty-caliber black powder guns."

"Gentlemen are there any questions?"

All I could do was stare! General Lance broke the silence. "Doctors, have you done the analysis of the lead marbles?"

Doctor Askin started right in. "Yes, we have a good estimate, but that is all. We have weighed the slag that has been found to date, estimated the slag scattered about on the countryside, and we estimate there were two tons of gold moved from Walnut Grove, Georgia, and stored under Yonder Rock at one time."

"How was all this gold moved?"

"We haven't explored the area under the crystalline rocks. We found one large wagon and a smaller one, but we were worried about a cave-in. We stopped exploration until further guidance."

I finally got my breath and asked, "At today's price, what would be the dollar amount?"

The doctors looked at each other, shrugged, and Doctor Askin spoke very distinctly, "We estimate there was over thirty-eight million dollars in gold bullion stored in Yonder Rock. We can account for two hundred eighty-eight troy ounces in storage at the present time. We know that Sam Feather spent twenty-eight troy ounces for the 155-millimeter projectiles. This leaves 47,184 troy ounces of gold unaccounted for. We don't have a clue where all that is gone. We believe the answer to transportation is buried with the two wagons that are in the upper chambers with all the hide bags."

I asked again how the doctors knew about the wagons. "We sent an unmanned camera into the upper chambers. About all we discovered were recent footprints in the dust. As we neared the wagons, we could see new wires connected to the crystalline rocks in some fashion. We stirred up so much dust, our camera lens became obscured. The camera is still in the area of the wagon, and we were afraid that a trap had been set and stopped investigating for the time being. General Lance, we didn't know what else to do for fear of compromising the inquiry."

To tell the truth, I had had about all my brain would handle, but no, the general was still captivated with the findings and was determined see the end. "Doctors, did you make a video of the camera's voyage into the chambers?"

"Yes, sir," said Doctor Brithen. "The batteries were running down, the dust got too thick, and we stopped progress."

"Okay, you did the right action by halting. I have a team assembled in Fort Sill that I will send you. They call them spelunkers; they specialize in close places and rock formations. Doctor Askin, I believe that is your specialty. You take charge of this phase and ferret out all the information that we can glean from this upper cave."

"They will have to bring all their equipment; we are limited in that area."

"Gentlemen, I believe we have had a very productive day. Chief Feather, I need to meet with you about this relation that has been disturbed."

"Yes, sir. Will we need to meet in my office tent, or would you want a walk around to clear our heads?"

General Lance and I didn't feel like being cooped up in a smelly tent and chose the river smells of nature. As we neared the muddy river water, I noticed a marked change in the general—relaxed, complacent with that far away look. "You know, Chief, I envy you and your people. You have held the secret of easy living for millennia and still get your aim in life done. As the doctors were presenting all of your linage today, you never showed any emotion. That doesn't alter your mission of deciphering the spirit circle. I need for this inquiry to wind down as soon as all the information is gleaned about your brother and his technique of spying with nothing but a bunch of eagle feathers and buffalo hide. I can see that there is more information about the lead marbles than we have found. Go ahead, ferret all the information you can get from your relatives in the name of seeking spirit circle data. In the name of government information, we can spend all the money we want to and nobody will ever know the difference. This conversation is private and not on record. Is that clear, Lone Feather?"

I noticed the general had called me by my given name. I appreciated that and answered, "Okay."

We returned to the present time. "Chief Feather, continue with my spelunkers. This bunch really knows their business, and the young recruits need the experience."

Spelunkers

The busload of the cave detectives arrived the next morning, all excited about the official outing. They fell in by my Black Hawk, and I gave them a field inspection. Chief Kindler presented them in camo fatigues; I introduced myself as Chief Feather. I told them that we do not salute while in the field except General Lance when he was in attendance. I set parameters of the work and turned them over to doctors Brithen and Askin. I saw a Gradall being unloaded and thought, *big toys for big boys.*

Their first project was to dig the wagon out of the upper grave chambers. This proved an easy way to trace the wiring of the crystalline formations. Each bucket of debris was examined by the doctors' crew, and I grew weary of all the operations. Surely there was something that I could do. I sat on the riverbank, watched the cranes squabbling over some fish kill, and watched the water swirl around the remains of Yonder Rock. Watching the water rise from some recent rain upstream, I became aware of gurgling up on the bank behind Yonder Rock and watched until my eyes fell asleep. I was jerked awake in a heartbeat. Gurgling behind me—this couldn't be—this is solid sandstone bank that runs all the way under the hillside.

This was a problem for Doctor Askin to unravel. I sent for the archeologist and held my ground to make sure I knew where the gurgling would manifest itself. Doctor Askin was talking to himself by the time he struggled down the river path. "Boy, boy, can't you find some path easier for me to come see you. Wow, Chief, I can hear what you are hearing. Is the river coming up?"

"Yes, the river is up at least a foot overnight, and from the looks of it, it will come up even more."

"We have been wondering how Miner got into the lower chamber, and you may have found a water-filled trap that was covered over in the explosion."

We called for help and soon uncovered the entrance of the water trap. "Okay, Mr. Chief, we want to be careful and not destroy any artifacts. Does your base have any flood control engineers?"

"Fort Sill has every known department that the United States Army has to offer. You describe to me what you want, and I can get it delivered to us."

"Have the engineers construct a coffer dam around the complete site out in the river by at least twenty feet, a mud pump to evacuate the mud and debris, a clean-up pump to pump river water so we can wash out the water trap, and several clean up tables. The spelunkers have brought scuba gear that should be sufficient to explore the cave's entrance."

General Lance readily agreed to the request and said he wanted a briefing as soon as the results were formulated. I watched the river as it receded back into its usual self, and we started another archeological phase. A scuba team came out of the caves and cleared the exit of the water trap of all rock that was deposited in the explosion. They could tell the water trap was full of all kinds of artifacts, so we waited for the engineers.

Doctor Askin

Our resident archeologists had three projects going at once. He chose to examine Auntie's house with a black light and Little Bird's and my help. The complete inside of her house glowed with that same purple glow, like the caves. We knew that Miner had spent many hours with his family, spreading the dye over everything he touched. We carried the long ammunition box down the stairs and completely categorized the contents. The overfilled hide box was put in a steamer in the examination rooms to soften the old hides. A Kentucky Long Tom Rifle was found that was completely worn out. All of the artifacts that pertained to Miner were displayed in the examination room for presentation. The excavation of the upper burial chambers revealed the two wagons, more miner tools, and lots of primer cord that was the same as Sam had used in the lower cave chambers. The doctors' remote camera was found and what seemed like an endless amount of hide bags. Doctor Brithen stopped examining the hide bags because the contents had been exposed to the elements so long there was nothing left but dust.

All the caves had been documented with full-color pictures, and it was determined that nothing was left of archeological value. Doctor Askin gave the spelunkers leave, and slowly all the heavy equipment was moved back to base. The engineers constructed the cofferdam, and the long-expected day came as we began pumping the mud and water. An unexpected surprise was the amount of flathead catfish that was caught in the cofferdam. All the experienced fishermen bailed into the fray, and our ole Arkie fixed us all the deep-pan-fried catfish we could eat. We had no idea that the mud of the Cimarron River was so slick, but the extra pump made short work of washing the old mud out. Both ends of the underground tunnel were washed out, and the explosion damage could be seen. A crew of rangers started finding the debris of centuries past, stone axes and arrowheads; the biggest surprise was the amount of round lead marbles, all fifty caliber. I had made an inventory of the lead marbles and put them all together in a safe place, in plain sight of the MPs. The doctors made their final reports, and we set a date for General Lance to receive the final briefing.

Briefing started with the doctor reports on the artifacts of Aunt Kildare's house. Miner Feather's MF was stamped on each tool. The lead marbles were from the mine that was found in the Walnut Grove, Georgia. Doctor Askin interjected that all the lead marbles had been cast from the same fifty-caliber mold. The exact mold was produced that showed a hairline crack on one side. All the marbles showed the crack, and it was surmised Miner had cast everyone from that mold.

The Kentucky rifle had the same lead residue found in the marbles and was most likely brought from Walnut Grove, Georgia, in 1811. A complete hiero-glyphic record was contained on the story hides, carbon dated to 1810. Doctor Askin gave the biggest news of the hour with a story hide of the stick figure of Miner Feather standing beside other stick figures of normal height. Yes, Miner was half the size, but with his floppy oversized hat. I thought the most interesting part was the picture of his small two-wheeled wagon. He had hold of the end gate with his right hand and a walking stick in his left hand. Doctor Brithen noted the square bones of the right hand of Miner and pointed out the position of him holding on to the end gate. The end gate of the small wagon was produced, and there was a hollow worn in the end of the gate.

"Gentlemen, the last years of Miner's life were fol-lowing the wagon and using the end gate to pull him along. The donkey bones we found in the graveyard excavation most likely was the donkey in the hide pictures. His notes mentioned L'ear and Big'ear. This leads us to believe there were two separate donkeys that pulled his wagon for more than 50 years. For the rest of the briefing we need to examine the wagons by the upper grave entrance."

I could see that General Lance was as enthralled as I was, and we eagerly looked forward to the end of this excursion. Doctor Askin told us about the cave acous-tics. "General Lance, I know you wanted the spirit circle to have a deep, dark secret revealed. All that I could find was a deep crystalline formation that runs almost to Fort Sill, Oklahoma. When I first saw the spirit circle in use, it did seem that a breakthrough had been discovered by Sam Feather for simple, long-range communications. This rock formation that we have dug out of the upper graves was installed by Sam Feather to pull us off the main path. He had pulled wire into the rocks and had connected them to the wagons. I have followed the formation, and he was off about ten feet in each mile. Yes, the spirit circle did work in a very narrow band, but it would be impossible to move several million tons of rock to set up a single listening post. The only real question is how Sam moved two wagons without destroying the whole hillside graveyard."

"Doctor Brithen, why did Sam want to listen in on our communications?"

"We have only begun to understand the effects of a lead-poisoned mind. Sam Feather had been trained with the Navy Seals, and his knowledge was extensive in listening devices. His mind was so twisted with those ideas, it consumed his inner being. You heard Little Bird's description of her husband when he had come out of the lower caves a raging animal, most likely as a result of breathing lead vapor in a closed space. Our opinion was that Sam, in his twisted mind, had to have those 155-millimeter projectiles. The only way he could get them was to melt the lead off of marbles and use the gold bullion on the international black market."

Doctor Askin picked up where Brethin left off. "Let's pay attention to the construction of a double bottom wagon that was most likely pulled by one of Miner's donkeys. This space contained bow and arrows, a long sword, and remnants of lead, all showing the same purple dye noted in the caves. Miner most likely distributed lead-covered gold to the tribes in Oklahoma. We have no proof outside the lead marbles we found in your Aunt Kildare Feather's house. It is my summation that Miner moved and gave away almost thirty-eight million dollars in today's prices of gold bullion over the fifty years he traveled in the Indian territories. I have run a series of population counts from 1812 until 1900. This central section of Oklahoma has more population than all the rest of the state combined. General Lance, in our summation, we feel that Miner Feather gave away his fortune to stabilize the deported Indians. This behavior is only seen in Christian families that wanted the people to survive.

"Mr. Chief, do you know of any contact the Feather clan had with Juan Ponca de Le'on?"

"The only record I have at this time is the 1811 land patent of Miner Feather. If I remember history, de Le'on came through the southeastern states around 1500."

"Yes, that is right, and that's why I asked you this question. We found a Spanish sword in the double bottom of the small wagon. That in itself is a miracle that we found it, but it is also in pristine condition. The only problem with it is the blood DNA from several men is found on the blade and handle. This DNA does not match any skeleton that we have in our examination room to date. We didn't know if Miner Feather was a swordsman or not. We revisited the Miner Feather skeleton the second time and found he had a large wound on the top of his head that was completely healed over. This put us on the trail of his big floppy hat; the top inch of his hat was completely cut off and sown back with fine stitches. Had we not turned the hat wrong side out, we wouldn't have found the repair. We found knife, axe, and lance wounds on the torso. Your great-great-grandfather was a hand-to-hand fighter, and all of his bone injuries were completely healed over. We have determined he never lost a fight, as he died of natural causes.

"It is our opinion Miner was the only person that ever knew about the gold-covered lead marbles until Sam Feather started melting the lead off of them about twenty-two months ago. For this, I feel that Doctor Brithen should do the presentation."

"Mr. Chief, this next portion is directed toward Sam Feather, your brother. We knew that Sam melted the lead off of the gold ingots in the kiln we found in the lower cave. We didn't know where Sam got the wood to fuel the kiln. In opening the upper cave, we discovered that hundreds of hide sacks and their contents were missing. The dust in the upper cave was very thick, being exposed to the elements for centuries. We found Sam's footprints in the dust that match the shoes he was found wearing when he died in the upper chamber. Gentlemen, it is our opinion that Sam used the hide bags and bones to fuel the kiln. We revisited the kiln and found bone, fat, and hide residue in the ashes. We don't have a clue as to who the bones belonged to, but the fact remains that the kiln needed a fuel source to melt the lead.

"Let's look at the bottom of the large wagon. At one time, it had a double bottom. It looks like all the gold-covered lead marbles were sealed in the cache, coated with animal fat to make the wagon float, and pulled by horses or mules 750 miles to Yonder Rock. How Miner Feather moved well over two tons of gold and lead into Yonder Rock is a mystery that we can't unravel. We have extrapolated that Miner made a hide bag that would hold enough lead marbles to hold him down in the cave water tunnel so he could walk on the bottom of the river and through the tunnel. We have studied modern-day Rangers that weigh around one hundred fifty pounds and could move that amount in a little over a year with the most up-to-date equipment. How Miner, without any scuba gear, could hold his breath that long is a mystery—and, oh, by the way—it is our estimation that Miner Feather didn't weight over sixty-five pounds with his three-foot-eleven frame."

"One last recommendation goes to Mr. Chief Feather," said Doctor Askin, "You have hired me to do a complete examination of the caves and rock formation. It is my opinion that you either set off a general explosion to relieve the pressure on the cave ceilings or get several helicopters to fly close to the ground so you get the same results. General Lance, this concludes my investigation, unless you have something else?"

"Doctor Askin, where do you want your pay sent?"

"If you don't mind, have it sent to the Alcohol Rehabilitation Center in Shawnee, Oklahoma. I'm a ward of the institution, and they handle all my finances." I thought, *Well, the ole boy has learned his lesson in life.*

General Lance nodded my way. "Chief Feather, when you are ready for the Apaches, call for an exercise on these coordinates. I'm sure my company will be more than glad to do a recon. Doctor Brithen, do you have any information that I need to hear?"

"No, except to Chief Feather. You have approximately eleven hundred pounds of gold covered with lead. It is my opinion that you not try to melt the lead down without a certified metallurgist and his safety equipment. You might wind up on my slab before you know it." I quickly looked his way and thought, *Yeah, right!*

General Lance and I had a private meeting to move all eleven hundred pounds of lead to the arms room at

Fort Sill, Oklahoma. My Black Hawk groaned with the added weight as I delivered its precious cargo to my old landing pad. A fork lift unceremoniously trundled my lead marked box to a top shelf. General Lance signed the papers and delivered the papers to my hand. As the gate slammed shut, the lights came on signaling that all was secure in the guard office. We breathed an eleven-million-dollar sigh and parted for the night.

EARLY OUT

Fort Sill got all the equipment back, including my Black Hawk helicopter, Humvee, spirit circle, computer, and all evidence were confiscated by the United States government for research. General Lance wanted me to sign up for another zillion years of active service, but this last jaunt seemed to be the early out excuse that I needed to retire with full Chief-4 status. I checked in all my service gear, signed all the necessary papers, and bid the Army adieu.

Something was nagging me to be with Little Bird. I had a lot of planning to do, and it all swirled around the old home place, our feelings toward each other, and what I could offer her. That little sprite had entwined within my mind, plans of the future, what I felt for her, the times our hands had touched seemed to sear out lives together. I felt we needed to sit down and reason this out, foot! I was in love with this girl and she needed to be told, NOW. I had been married to the army so long, they told me what and where to jump, my whole being was military. Now, now I can't figure what to do!

I did make myself get transportation with my severance pay. A new yellow Hummer seemed to fit my frame, and I broke it in on the way home. I blistered I-35 all the way north and straightened out Hy-33 to the Euchee Creek turnoff.

Traveling to my section of land seemed to take an entire day from Fort Sill. As I neared Sam's old house, there was Dog baying his head off. That seemed strange, and then I heard Little Bird's voice way off. "Lone Feather, come get me! Hurry, I'm stuck in the upper chambers." I rushed up the hill and heard the ground moaning. "Hurry, Lone, my foot is stuck under a rock." I grabbed a shovel and ran into the cave. I had to come back out for the dust and rock that was falling. "Loooooone, come quick!"

I will get Little Bird out or die trying. "Little Bird, keep talking so I can find you." A brown blur swept by my legs as Dog charged into the cave. Another moan-groan swept through the cavern's interior. I fell pell-mell through the gathering darkness, heard Dog whine, and reached the interior of the rockslide. My shovel was worthless in the small places; I tore at the rocks, holding Little Bird with my bare hands. A slight movement was felt in the strata, and Little Bird slipped into my arms. All I could think of was finding the entrance, fresh air, sunlight. We stumbled to safety as the slabs of sandstone slid over each other. Another lurch and the whole of the hillside settled onto the cave floors. We looked on as the trees slid sideways and settled at slanted angles—more groans as the cave system twisted itself downhill into the Cimarron River.

We lay in the hot summer sun until the noise and dust settled onto our sweating bodies. I tenderly felt of Little Bird's swollen ankle; I knew she was still alive from the dust-choked cough. Where Dog came from I will never know, but there he was lying beside us. I felt of this whimpering dog and thought, *I wonder if I would have ever found Little Bird had it not been for that hound.* We loaded up in the Hummer and made for the Cimarron River. I had remembered my early training that the red mud was good for scrapes and bruises. I stopped in running water and gave all of us a good splashing bath. Little Bird's ankle was a sprain; Dog and I had multiple bruises most likely from falling rock.

Little Bird turned into a mess of sobs. "Oh Lone, I'm sorry, please forgive me, I'm so sorry, I could have gotten all of us killed, I'm so sorry."

"Wait, Little Bird, why are you so sorry? I have been gone and left you here all by yourself. Little Bird, why were you in the caves?"

"Oh Lone, the people, the people were looking for gold. They come at all hours poking around in the caves. I tried to find it and save it for you."

"Let's go to your house, change clothes, and put an Ace bandage on your ankle. I want to show you something."

We found Auntie's old house site intact, but it was as if all the past years had been erased and started with an all new day. My old place seemed so peaceful after all the turmoil; there was no evidence of Yonder Rock. Huge slabs of new sand stone jetted out in its place.

The new Hummer would take us to any spot on the river we wanted to go. A stop in the running water seemed to be the best.

"Little Bird Feather, there is something on my mind; we have walked around each other too long and lets get something straight. I'm in love with you and want to be around you more and more, do you feel anything for me?"

"Lone, when I saw you the first time with your army personnel, it was as if Sam had been healed of his craziness, and I was to be whole again. That turned out to be a big disappointment on my part; I wanted to blame you for killing my husband. I wanted to hate you for destroying my life, but as reason prevailed I saw that you were a victim, the very same as I. Yes, there is something between you and me. I felt it today as you cared for me. I have a long way to go before the Lord can heal my heart from my loss. Give me time and space to make up my own mind, and if something comes of this experience, I say let it be."

"I have been in the same quandary as you, only military. I lived, breathed, spoke, thought, dreamed—my whole being army. Today is the first time that my mind has done anything different. I held your body and I agree with this experience. I say let it grow.

"Little Bird you mentioned the gold, this is an arms receipt for eleven hundred pounds of lead/gold held for my use only. When we are ready, I will have the lead melted off and convert all that gold bullion into bank notes."

"Oh, Lone."

LONE AND LITTLE BIRD

Little Bird and I couldn't stay away from each other, so we made a trip into Cushing, stood before the justice of the peace, said our vows, and became married in the fall. We walked over the home place, dug where we wanted, ran through the woods, and swam in the murky waters of the Cimarron River. We planned out a lifetime of building the old home place to its original status. We tried, but our plans never seemed to last very long. All our folks were gone, the landslide had covered all the old caves, and really, we were in a foreign land. We tried to set up housekeeping amongst all the old memories. We moved into Sam's hide teepee and stayed one night. If we had to live outside under the stars, it would have been better than sleeping with animal hides on all sides. We even stayed in a motel a night or two, ate out at the fast food restaurants, and made a beeline back home. Bird and I decided that we were spoiled brats and liked the white man's way of living and would never go back two hundred years.

We moved into Aunt Kildare's house the second time and decided to read the journal of Miner Feather, maybe trace all the dots on his map. We made another trip into town and bought a large motor home, set up housekeeping on the old home place, and tried to settle down. Yes, this did have a plan to it, and the journal came alive with the map. Our first excursion was around the river, down off the high bluffs, and we found nothing! We couldn't find one site that looked like a settlement. On to the next, nothing—maybe some pottery shards. We must have looked at a dozen sites and only found some ole campfire clumps. We were doing something wrong, but what? After a month of looking around the Cimarron River bluffs, we all but gave up on ever finding anything. We camped, parked, and lived for the day we could find any of our past.

Our next excursion was to town to catch a few garage sales and mull over what we were doing wrong. We found out that when you live in a motor home, you don't collect very much baggage. We had taken the Hummer, and I was just watching, listening to the radio, bored stiff. Bird was doing her garage sales bit. For some reason, I was attracted to a display and found a jar full of marbles. They were marked fifty cents, and I offered a quarter and took my marbles home with us. As with all finds, when you are looking for something, always look in the unexpected places. Bird and I decided to play a game of marbles when we got back to the sandy beach. I was giving her half, and I poured a fifty-caliber lead ball out in her hand! All I could say was "Gag!"

"Bird, let's go back to town and see if there are any more of these marbles."

"Why?"

"I think it's time you knew the complete story about Miner Feather, don't you?"

"Oh, I don't think so. My memories are so terrible about that time."

"Okay, but we have to go back and find out about this lead ball and buy a battery-powered black light."

Our trip back to town seemed to take forever. As we pulled up to the garage sale, they were quitting for the day. "Pardon me," I asked. "Do you have any more of these lead marbles?"

"We don't know. Poppa found that out on the Cimarron River before he died. He would have liked to have found more but never did."

"When did he find this one?"

"Oh gosh, I don't know. He was always poking around that old bridge that used to be over the river and came home with it one day. It must have been twenty-five or thirty years ago. Why, do you think there are more?" I could see this wasn't getting anywhere and excused myself. "Young man, Poppa always thought it might be something that went with a gun some way, but it's all over now." I said that I was sorry to bother her, and Bird and I went on our way.

We found a portable black light, got a bucket of chicken, and headed for the ole homestead. I waited until dark, got out the black light, and our hands shone like old time purple. Bird tried to rub the dye off and had purple pockets, purple all over ourselves, the Hummer, the lead marble. "Bird, watch this." I rolled the marble over the tailgate and all it could do was wobble.

"Lone, honey, I think it's time you tell me the complete story!"

"This story is too strange not to be true. Let's use the Hummer, take a river bath, and I will start the story of Yonder Rock."

I took us down to some shallow water and turned the black light on. We had to take a good splashing bath. Bird couldn't get over the effects of the salt water on the purple dye. I washed the lead marble completely clear of any purple. As the story unfolded, Bird became more and more involved. We made plans to start completely over with the hunt for our past.

We decided to live nocturnally, and hunting with the black light at night turned out to be a real treasure trove. Miner's map would show us a general location of the clans that we were hunting. The night scope maps that I had taken earlier from the Black Hawk showed us the long extinct trails and the lead slag that was spread by Miner. Our first location to search was east of us by two miles. We pulled the Hummer behind the motor home and set out to find the past. All we could do was get close and walk the rest of the way. We walked in and found a few specks of light but nothing of value; we could tell that Miner had been there two hundred years ago. As we neared our motor home, we could tell that we had company in the form of the local police car. We sauntered up and asked if we could help in any way.

The police met us at the fence line and shone their light in our eyes. "Oh foot, Pete, this is a pair of Indians on Indian land. We don't have a case here."

"What was the problem?"

"Son, we have a report of somebody going in on Indian land looking for gold. I can see you were having a picnic in those old ruins. In the future, be sure you call ahead and tell us you are in these sacred grounds, and we won't bother you."

I introduced myself and Bird. I thanked them and wanted to know who had turned us in. "Oh, Mr. Anthony Ables of the BIA has a standing order to arrest any whites that trespass on Indian land. We were making our nightly cruise when we saw your motor home and could see lights coming back from those ole Indian ruins."

"Officer, is there a form we can make out so we won't have this problem again?"

"Sure, come to my squad car. Let me run a spot check, and I'll make you out a sticker you can put in the windshield of your motor home."

Boy, what luck we will have—thousands of square miles to track Miner's travels. We signed up that night to hunt all those old trails and got a purpose to see our history. Our Hummer took us back to town, and I bought a metal detector to help us out on the old camp sights. On our next excursion, we found a very poor clan squatting on Indian land. Bird got out the story hide and tried to reason with the occupants. Nothing.

A very old gruff voice came out of the house and said, "Bring the story hide up on the porch. I want to see it."

Only then did we notice the wrinkled old man sitting with a blanket over his shoulders. Bird did the talking, and the old brave brightened up and asked the question. "Are there any of the Feather clan still living?" I introduced myself as Lone Feather Jr. and found out his name was Two Bear Jones. "Lone, what was your relation to Miner Feather?"

"My great-great grandfather was Miner Feather. I am the last relation alive that we can find of that clan. Look on the story hide at his picture. I have several miner tools that are marked MF." I could see the tears running down the old brave's cheeks as he talked to his clan to bring out their story hide. His hide almost mirrored my version down to the wagon and donkey. As always, Miner had that big floppy hat on.

We shared our stories that day. Two Bear thanked the Feather clan for furnishing food when they were starving. He couldn't get over that we would look them up after all these years. "Two Bear, how old are you?"

"Oh, I don't know, but I remember your great-grandfather, Wounded Nose. How about his wife, Kildare? Is she still alive?"

"Great Aunt Kildare is gone. We buried her just a short time ago." I asked again about Miner Feather. Did he ever see him?

"No, I never saw him, but I remember my poppa telling about the little ole man that wandered these hills, giving away whatever was in his wagon."

"I want to show you something and see if you can remember having any of them." I pulled a lead marble out of my pocket, and you should have seen the change in the old brave's face.

"Do you have any more shot? We have run completely out and can't hunt any more. Boys, bring out my Kentucky rife. Maybe we can shoot something to eat." The rifle matched the one found in Yonder Rock cave.

"Two Bear, how many of these lead marbles did you have?"

"I don't know. Miner left us with plenty to hunt game, but we shot them up and could never buy any more."

"Where did you shoot them the most?"

"See that Bois D'Ark tree out there, about fifty yards? It's a wonder the old thing didn't die of lead poisoning from all the lead that is in its bark."

As Bird and I took our metal detector out to the tree, I wondered then if we should tell them about all the gold they had shot through that Kentucky rifle. It was as Two Bear has said—the tree was completely dead on the house side. My metal detector went wild at this find; we couldn't count the gold-lead slugs that were embedded under the bark. We did show the clan what Miner had given them with the hopes they could handle the cash flow that would come.

Bird and I took our burden on to the next spot on the map. As it happened, the river had moved and completely washed the campsite down river. We took our metal detector and scanned the side of the hill. The black light shown at night told the old story of Miner's visits with the tribes. We found three lead balls and felt good about knowing that we were on the right track. Whom the balls belonged to we never found out. We found more at night then at day with the black light, and the hunt was on.

The map didn't have any towns marked, but we did find an old trading post within reach of my home place. A trip to the courthouse told that a Mexican had owned the land, and that was about all. There were no current records or deeds for the last hundred years. We waited until dark, and the black light lit up the complete floor of the trading post. Maybe, just maybe, we had found the post mentioned in the journal. We had to find the current owners. The courthouse again noted that the last owners were dead and the place was for sale, if I would pay the taxes. I cautiously asked how much, and the answer scared us. One hundred dollars and they would quit claim the deed to me. Another six dollars registered the deed, and we were in possession of a pile of hand-hewed logs and a lot of purple dye!

Bird and I started the next day with setting our camper on the lot, putting up yellow Keep Out tape around the hillside, and getting to see a zillion cars go by with people shaking their heads.

Those Indians are going to build another casino. Hum-mph—just let them believe that while we are searching for gold! I rented a backhoe, dug several test holes, tore down some old scrub oak trees, parked the hoe in plain sight of the road, and then got on with our main objective: looking for lead balls.

Our night excursions with the black light proved that Miner had indeed spent considerable time staying with the man we only knew as Tex-mix. Our first project was ordering out a large roll-off Dumpster, cleaning out the trash of two centuries ago, and going through each item from the old log store. We took the store building apart piece by piece, examined, and ran the black light on everything. We didn't find much until we got to floor level. Miner must have sat on the end of the porch, and his friend sat on a chair leaned back against the wall. The floor was almost completely worn through from the chair. Where Miner sat was black, greasy, and full of lead slag particles, the purest purple that glowed under the black light. We found our first lead marble under a knot hole, then gold flakes by the handful under the sitting end of the porch. Little Bird bagged all the soil in with the gold flakes for future examination. I don't know how many coins I found that had fallen through the cracks at the front door, with as many buttons, safety pins, and of all things, a lady's garter. We wondered how she kept her hose up. "Oh, Lone, keep your mind on you own business."

The floor of the store was just a mass of holes that had been patched with flat sheet tin, jar lids, and spare boards that were most likely wore out before they were nailed down with square nails. We pondered this and couldn't remember any patches like that in the modern stores. We found where the flour, corn, beans, and cracker barrels sat; the space under the floor was completely full of the products from the barrels.

Bird and I spent days cleaning the store out, taking the old notched logs down, and chinking by the bucketfuls. Then we sifted all the dust to making sure we didn't miss anything. The Dumpster received all this without complaint. We weren't satisfied until we got to the back door and the outside shed. The shed turned out to be the stable for the donkeys. We used the black light and could only get a trace. Our black light kept shining that purple glow around the back door. We had found where Miner stopped his wagon and unloaded and repacked his trade goods. We began to find flakes of gold that looked like it had been cut off of the marbles. We didn't show this to anybody, just kept bagging everything so we could get it back to base camp. Our drive-through company only looked at the torn up mess in the back lots and that backhoe standing guard with its boom outstretched and the bucket as high as it would go. People wanted something to look at, talk about, and we furnished plenty of ideas.

Our search finally drew to an end; I filled all the dirt holes, stacked the log building, and burnt the lot. As soon as the fire was out, I dug another hole, buried all the ashes with fresh dug dirt, and left the drive-by company to wonder what those Indians were up to next. The Dumpster Company made the last tracks, and we went home the short way to sift through our gold flakes.

I got out Miner's old kiln and remembered how Doctor Brithen had warned me to put a flue pipe above my head and started right in melting my gold ore down in small ingots. My first trial was just that; I spilt the whole mess in the sand. My next batch was at least poured into a cast-iron cup. I couldn't imagine how flowing gold was so luxurious looking. Bird and I run the little foundry all our waking hours. As we were working, we talked about how crazy my brother Sam became from working the gold. We could well understand the mood he would get into. The smoke would carry off all the noxious fumes, and we melted gold into several ingots. I took the kiln completely apart when we finished. I didn't trust anybody knowing what we were doing and took the ingots to our safe deposit box.

We wandered back to Two Bear's house and found a calamity had torn the family asunder. They had taken the tree completely apart to get the slugs of gold out, sold the gold on the black market, and tried to drink up the better part of three thousand dollars of whisky. This taught Bird and me a lesson: don't give gold to our fellow man. We would think of another way to give it away, but not drink.

CIMARRON MISSION

Our next dot destination was marked CM. We took the motor home and Hummer to the Pawnee, Oklahoma, RV park, set up camp, and slept the clock around. The excursion at Tex-Mix's store was a mite much, so we took some time off and explored the sleepy town. We didn't find anything that looked like Miner had been there; even the black light didn't show anything, our best time to hunt was at night. We looked ourselves blind and never saw a shine of purple until we got to the drainage ditches. Just a few specks of purple, then nothing, then a few more, just enough to keep our interest up. Phooey on that nighttime staring into the dark. We moved our search to the daylight. The drainage ditches were in the old part of the park with the back of the business toward the ditch. We for sure couldn't see in the daylight, so back to the black light at night. Our search took us past an old stone building, and we lost the specks. By backtracking, we felt the stone building had some meaning to the search. Search we did the next day and found a church building that was run-down, and we thought unused, until an old gent came out, shook a rug, then returned to his labors inside.

We gave up for the day and heard church bells the next morning coming from the stone building. We dressed for church and attended the morning mass of the Cimarron Missions to the Indians. We couldn't believe our luck that day; we found the CM and praised the Lord with the parishioners. We didn't mention it to anybody but went back after dark that night to make sure we were in the right place.

Oh, we found all kinds of purple coming from under the floor and were found out also by the town police. The patrol car came to our motor home, introduced himself as Police Chief Sims of the Pawnee tribe, and asked our names. I told him the truth—that we were Lone and Little Bird Feather from the Cherokee tribe. He then asked me a question that we never expected, "Mr. and Mrs. Feather, did you find the gold at the old mission?"

I know we looked guilty as our faces fired that certain red color and tried to stammer some explanations. The police chief smiled and told us a story that runs through the mission every few years. "At one time, two centuries ago, this mission had all kinds of gold. Where it came from and where it went, they never knew. Somewhere around 1860, the gold stopped coming and the old mission is just that now—*old*. We watch over the mission, and we know all the cars coming and going through town. Now, when your motor home was parked here in the RV Park and you show up with a yellow Hummer, you are a marked couple. Folks,

I wouldn't want anything to happen to our Father Knowins. You are welcome to worship with us anytime you can. We have your tag numbers, and I knew who you were before I came to you motor home. You gave me the right answers. Now, Lone, what is your business with that black light? Why did the purple specks show up around the floor of this church?"

Little Bird and I looked at each other and right there decided we needed some help from Chief Sims. "Chief, we are here on a fact-finding tour of a relative of mine named Miner Feather."

"*Stop*, don't tell me you are some relation to Miner Feather."

"I am the great-great-grandson of Miner Feather." I got my paper signed by Doctor Brithens that stated that indeed I was that grandson.

"Lone Feather, please excuse me. I have to check this out. Come out to my cruiser while I make some telephone calls." I witnessed a very excited police chief talk to Doctor Brithen. He told the chief about the black light showing the purple dye, the connection with lead, and Miner Feather.

We swore each other to secrecy that night and that nothing was to be done without all of us meeting with Father Knowins. A meeting was set up for the next morning, and I took my black light to make sure what we had was proof positive. Father Knowins was a kindly gentleman of the cloth and made us feel comfortable. Chief Sims told about us being in town and that I was the great-great grandson of Miner Feather. It was as if a light had been turned on in the priest's face.

"Yes, in the church archives, we have a Miner Feather as a charter member of the Cimarron Mission. In fact, he helped build this very building. I believe it describes your grandfather as being a slight-built man that could out work any grown man. It even describes his wagon and donkey that hauled sand from the creek bottom for mortar on these very rocks."

I got out my story hides that showed stick figures of Miner. There was no doubt that all the stories were true. "Now, Chief Sims and Father Knowins, I have something to show you, and I want to run a black light test on the inside of the sanctuary and vicarage. Have you seen any of these lead balls?"

Chief Sims was the first to speak. "That looks like a rifle ball for some of those old black powder guns."

"Yes, this peculiar one is a fifty caliber."

Father Knowins nodded and said, "Gentlemen, I believe we have a bucket of those down in the basement somewhere. If you will accompany me, we will search."

All Little Bird and I could do was shake our heads at what was about to develop. We followed the good shepherd down a long span of stairs and watched as the bucket of gold balls covered with lead was produced. "Chief Sims, now you will see the black light in use." A strange purple glow emitted from the bucket, a slow stream of purple water could be seen dotting the floor to an outside drain.

"Chief, when you talked to us last night, you asked about the purple specks outside in the drainage ditch. I have found the source of the dye with this black light. This is the way we find where Miner Feather has been. In fact, gentlemen, look at the wall of this basement. These are the specks from his clothing. Father, you are right, Miner helped build these very walls. In fact, he helped support this church for almost two hundred years. I have cut into one of these balls for you to examine."

"Oh my goodness!" exclaimed the men in unison. "Lone, you mean to tell me we have had all this gold for almost two hundred years and didn't know it?"

"Yes, Father, you have, and now I want to warn you that the lead on the outside of these marbles is very toxic but can be melted off, and you will have pure gold. You should have enough here to build another church building."

"Oh, my son" spoke the father, "we have been searching for God's will for so long, and this is the answer to our prayers. Brother Sims, what say ye on this matter?"

"We have a metal worker in our congregation that can handle melting this down and the bank of Tulsa can help us convert all gold to cash. We can afford to put the stone structure back in shape, maybe for another two hundred years. Lone and Little Bird Feather, how much do we owe you for finding all this?"

We looked at each other and I spoke for both of us. "Father Knowins and Police Chief Sims, we think you have the situation well in hand. Go with your plans at hand. This is our aim, to follow in the footsteps of my great-great grandfather, Miner Feather, and help the people to wake up to what they have. It is my opinion that Miner gave this lead-covered gold as an offering to the Lord as it was needed. Somewhere in the giving, the word was lost to melt the lead off, and people thought that they were getting lead balls to be shot through a Kentucky fifty-caliber rifle. We don't want anything for our services; we want the gold used to the glory of the Lord and nothing else. Chief we could use several days to get out of the territory before somebody thinks we're after gold."

"I can do something better than that. You get all ready to go, and I will escort you like I'm escorting a criminal out of town like all the other gold seekers."

We followed that blinking bubble gum machine over the next hill and gave each other a gentle wave as we parted.

Our next point on the map was by far the most enjoyable. We traveled at night and pulled into a park by the name of Mannford Ramp. It was a moonless night, and we woke up the next morning just before noon. Little Bird squealed like a banshee and started jerking drawers open until she found our bathing suits. I was still enjoying my soft pillow when I heard her make the first splash in the swimming area. We had pulled into the best camping spot on the lake and didn't even know where we were. I moped myself around and splashed with that water sprite until we were hungry as bears. A trip to the golden arches solved that problem. A boat rental fitted us with a ski rig, and we spent the day plying the waters of Keystone Lake. We couldn't believe the red Cimarron River could be cleared enough to ski in, much less swim.

A good night's rest put us on the trail of Miner. I had marked the spot on our map, but everything had been changed. We finally figured out the clan's location was covered with one hundred feet of water. All we could do was shrug our shoulders and move to the next spot. We took the ski rig back and found a pawnshop next door. Well, what the heck, let's slum the joint. After seeing all the overpriced guns, lanterns, knives, bicycles, and nonessentials, we wound up at the glass-covered case to admire the rings and watches. Little Bird very timidly pointed out three lead balls that looked the right size for a large rifle. I asked how much, and the pointy-faced kid said they were rifle balls, three for ten dollars. A closer examination proved they were the right size, a roll down the counter told me the wobbling story I wanted to see. I paid the price and asked if there were any more. He frowned and said that he didn't know and to come back tomorrow and see his dad.

"Son, where did you get these lead marbles?"

"Sir, my gramps picked up all the arrowheads and these marbles before the lake filled up."

We knew we were at the right location but couldn't do anything about it.

GRASSLANDS

We decided to turn north and try some of the dots north of Yale, Oklahoma. We sat the motor home down, and the Hummer was much easier to get around the old oil patches. We had a dot at Maramec and Quay, but there weren't many peoples left after the oil boom. Jennings was a little better, so we stopped at a farm ranch and asked if anybody knew about a Miner Feather from years ago and were told in no uncertain terms to hit the road.

We were almost in our Hummer when an old, bow-legged feller came out and apologized for his grandson's remarks. He asked, "Why you trying to stir up old Indian trouble?"

I told him my business and that we were trying to find a clan of Indians that my grandfather knew at one time. "Oh, is that right, son? You better be from the Feather clan to ask questions like that."

"Yes, that is exactly who I am. My name is Lone Feather, Jr."

Old Bow Legs looked at me real close and admitted that yes, I was from that clan, he could see the resemblance. "Tell you what, Lone, you bring your wife and let's go set on the porch and talk about this tie."

Mr. Bow Legs limped back to the rocking chair and motioned for us to help ourselves to the ones we liked. His next remarks were in the dialect of the Cherokee language. I don't know what he said, but he got the job done in less time than it takes to tell it. We had fresh iced tea, a picture book, and a very embarrassed young man standing in front of us.

"Mr. Lone Feather, I'm sorry for the way I talked when you drove up. We thought you were one of the tourists that wanted to take pictures of us Indians. We get our share."

"Son, I'm sorry I talked to you like I did. I think we should forget about all this and find out if we're some shirttail relation. By the way, son, what is your name?"

The young man stood his full four feet tall and spoke in perfect English. "Sir, my name is One Feather." *I couldn't believe what I had just heard!*

"Lone, we need to get one thing clear. Are you any relation to Miner Feather?" Bow Legs asked. I excused myself and got my briefcase and pulled out the linage line made by Doctor Brithen and gave it to him. More Cherokee and out came a set of glasses to ole Bow Legs. Absolute quiet prevailed until a sob came from under his hat. "Lone Feather, we share the same great-great grandfather in Miner Feather. My name is Jim Feather. We are some kind of cousins three or four generations back." By then, Little Bird and I were sitting, amazed at the turn of events. We had stumbled on close relations from two hundred years ago.

"Where do you live?" Jim asked.

"I live on the old home place where Miner Feather settled in 1811. Little Bird and I are traveling around in our motor home, trying to fit the clans back together since the deportation of Indians from Walnut Grove, Georgia."

"Stop the telling. We have got to get all my family together so they can hear all this at one time. What are you and your wife doing for the next week or so?"

"We are footloose and trying to get our family history straightened out."

"Okay, go get your motor home and park it around back of our house. I will get on the horn and gather all my family together this next weekend, and we'll have us a powwow of the Feather clan."

"I see you have picture albums. If I bring a computer and printer, can we copy each other's pictures?"

"You bring anything you want, and we'll put all this together."

Little Bird and I couldn't believe our good luck finding Jim's family so easily. During the trip back to the grasslands around Jennings, we began to notice more and more fine racing horses. We pulled into Jim Feather's ranch before dark and did as he said—picked out a RV spot on the top of the hill. There must have been fifty connections, and we were the only one. Here were complete paddock facilities, hay barns, show barn, and kids running everywhere. We couldn't count the horses of all sizes and colors. We wondered then if we were intruding on somebody else's ranch. My Uncle Jim didn't seem like he should have this many facilities.

Here came One on a bay horse that looked like it came from a show ring. "Lone Feather, come over to the chow hall, the pizza just got here."

"Little Bird, I wonder what I have got us into. This is a ritzy layout, and One mentioned pizza."

"I think we should dress in jeans and boots for this western shindig." We scrambled into our old jeans, red flannel shirts, and old bolo ties and joined at least fifty of the Feather Clan.

"Lone, you and Little Bird get at the head of the line, and we'll bless the food and get started." Jim waited until everybody was quiet and spoke reverently. "People of the Feather clan, this is Lone and Little Bird Feather. Lone and I share the same great-great-grandfather, Miner Feather." I heard a gasp come from the crowd and could feel fifty pairs of eyes trained on us. "Lone is going to be with us, and I want all of you to thank him and his wife for looking us up. Most of you know what Miner means to us and the surrounding clans of Indians. Now this is Saturday night, and I want all of you to be in church and Sunday school tomorrow. I'm going to see to it that each one of you gets good Christian upbringings, just like Grandpa wanted. Now, let's all bow our heads for the blessing, and then it is up to you to show us how you like pizza."

All I can say is we ate like Feathers that evening; the pizza lasted just long enough to get us ready for the Saturday night races. Little Bird was called to the front with five other young married women. They let them draw for horses and took them out to the show barns. We all rushed to the bleachers to see the first race of the evening. The typical Indian race was around the poles twice and back to the starting line. I had no idea that Little Bird could even ride, much less race, until she got her mount straightened out by the second pole. There was another slim girl neck and neck with her, with her hat tied down tight. Little Bird won by decision, and the spectators exploded in joy. Guess who was called on next?

Several of us men were pulled out of the crowd, put on saddled broncos, a flag was dropped, and all the mounts exploded into a bucking frenzy. I'm sure I was the first one to get a mouth full of *stuff* from the racetrack. Laugh, but you should have seen the Indians laying out in the grass, hooting the evening. I couldn't count the races that we had. The horses were switched every few minutes so we could have fresh mounts. Little Bird rode again and lost; everybody got to win at least once.

My cell phone went off as we were about run down. "Chief Feather, what are you doing in Jennings, Oklahoma, this time of the night?"

"General Lance, where are you?"

"I'm on my monthly night flight. I've got my own cell phone and decided to give you a shout. We triangulated your signal, and I'm about ten minutes away from you."

"You know the offer you gave me to send a squadron of Apaches to fly over my old home place to vibrate the ceilings down?"

"Yes, Chief, I suppose you want me to land in that circle of light up ahead."

"Affirmative, General Lance, and let me borrow your helmet. I want to give a friend a ride." I corralled Jim and told him to clear the arena. We could hear the Black Hawk's flop-flop coming, and I had the attention of plenty of Feathers that night. They didn't have a clue what was coming as General Lance set down and jumped out.

I strolled out to my old general, saluted right smart, and he gave me my old helmet and said he figured I would need it in time. I put my helmet on, climbed into my old Black Hawk, got the loudspeaker going, and made the announcement that Jim Feather was to board my helicopter. They had to drag the old Indian out and stuff him in the passenger seat. I called for all the young Indian braves to load up in the cargo hold. We took a midnight ride, courtesy of the United States government. I set back down after a fifteen-minute ride, as all the little braves were kind of green around the gills. I gave my helmet back to the government, shook hands with my old general, and sent him on his way. Jim told me later we were even for the joke of the bucking broncos. We both hugged each other and got ready for the Lord's Day tomorrow.

I don't think that my wife slept very much that night from bragging about how she could still ride with the wind. I brushed my teeth twice and could still smell something that smelled like a horse! Sunday church was a real victory celebration for the Lord. This played us out so much; we had to take afternoon naps. I was the main speaker after the snoring stopped. I told of the family connection that Jim Feather and I shared and how Miner gave of himself to help the clans survive the deportation. I told of the Cimarron River and all the people that were buried there, how the caves had all collapsed, and the miracle of Little Bird getting out alive.

Jim took over, told how Miner had helped them and asked, "Was there anybody there that couldn't forgive all the injustices?" Silence prevailed as Jim led us

in a closing prayer to end the weekend. Jim broke in
with, "Now don't anybody leave; the burgers are coming from the golden arches."

We had the winner's circle go through first, and you
should have seen those young Indians go through the
line. Jim and I got our share and sat away from those
screamers so we could continue our talk. "I guess you
can see how the Lord had blessed us. Just think how all
this got started."

"Did Miner set your family up on this horse
ranch?"

"No, as a matter of fact, all he ever gave my great-
grandfather One was help getting a large parcel of the
grass prairie from the Pawnee Indian tribe. Miner took
his son One, and they went to the Pawnee headquarters and filed on four sections of grassland. I have the
original land patent at home in my name. We didn't
know at the time where the gold came from to buy all
this. We always thought that the gold that was given to
the Cherokee Tribe for land had found its way to One
some way. I didn't know.

"Years and years ago, oil was discovered on our land,
and you can see the rest of the puzzle. We had a grandfather, Wounded Nose, that didn't want anything to do
with grassland. All these holdings have fallen into my
control. I have invested all the excess, and we live off of
the interest. As far as I know, all my family will never
want for money of any kind. Do you and Little Bird
need money?"

I thought about not telling Jim about the Miner
legacy and thought again, *Somebody in our family needs
to understand, and this will be a good place to start.*

"I need to tell you about the story that has run in
our family for almost two hundred years. Miner, our

great-great-grandfather's family owned a lead mine in Walnut Grove, Georgia. Miner was making all sizes of rifle balls to be shot through the black powder guns of the age. In fact, I have found all of Miner's tools. Ball molds, which they used to make and sell the rifle balls—all of these molds are marked MF.

"After the Louisiana Purchase of 1803, the United States government wanted to deport any disruptive Indians to the Indian Territory, later to be called Oklahoma. Since Miner's lead mine started producing gold, a huge problem developed for them to be caught moving large amounts of gold. Miner devised a lead-covered gold ball that could be shot thru a .50 Caliber gun. He made a false bottom for a Conestoga wagon to conceal at least two tons of lead-gold balls. The Miner's clan decided to move around 1810, to not be in the push of 1838 known as the Trail of Tears. Jim, I want to show you one of these marbles and you tell me if you have ever seen anything like it."

I showed Jim a lead marble, and he didn't have any interest but did go to his safe and got one of his marbles out that matched mine.

"We discovered the secret of the lead marbles when I was kid by shooting them through a rifle. I don't know how many we wasted until we found out they were gold covered with lead, but the rest of them bought many a head of racehorses. I think I'm about to learn where the gold came from. Are there any more in existence?"

"That's exactly what Little Bird and I are trying to find out. We have found them in abundance in strange places. Most people don't have a clue what they have, and if you tell them, they are likely to try to drink themselves under the tables. Jim, you are the third man that has discovered the real truth of the lead-covered gold marbles. Little Bird and I have found them, mostly by accident, and not many people have discovered the real meaning of Miner's legacy except you.

"Jim, our great-great grandfather moved two tons of gold covered with lead from Georgia to the old home place in 1811. He was a miner and knew how to melt the lead off of the marbles, then converted the gold to staple goods and gave away most of his fortune in the years he traveled this very land, trading beans and corn to his fellow men. I have his journal from all those years, and his last entry was August 20, 1863. Jim, I have found enough gold to amount to eleven million dollars to date. Now Jim, do you need any money?"

"No, Lone, I don't. The Lord has blessed our efforts to serve him so much, and we have all that we want. You mentioned that our peoples try to drink up their assets. Why do our fellow Indians try to destroy their lives that way?"

"It's not only the Indians, but people of all races have that problem."

Jim and I started the next day with his picture albums. We don't know who took the tintypes of 1858, but there was our great-great-grandfather looking out from under his big floppy hat. My printer got a work-out that day, spitting out those full-page prints of our ancestry. Jim called his son One Feather; they spoke in Cherokee, which left me out. It wasn't long before in strolled the modern version of Miner Feather, in the same big floppy hat with that mischievous grin on his face. I took several full-color shots of One, entered them in my computer, overlaid the black and white of Miner with One's color. I printed them off and had a 2008 print of One and Miner standing side by side.

You would have thought they were brothers, not separated by two hundred years.

I gave One copies of the doctor's inquiry about all the skeletons of our ancestry. It took him an entire day to understand the doctor's jargon, but he had an all-new insight about the olden days. He understood why he was so short, and as far as I know, never asked about it anymore. We made plans to attend the Feathers' powwow each year, and they in turn promised to visit the old home place and swim in the Cimarron River. Little Bird and I left the Jim Feather clan full with the knowledge that Miner's legacy was being fulfilled in the Lord.

LAST OF DOCTOR ASKIN

My cell phone began buzzing to the song "Wild Thing."
"Hello?"

"Is this Mr. Chief Feather?"

"Yes," I stammered.

"This is Miss Servers of the Alcohol and Rehabilitation center in Shawnee, Oklahoma. We have a missing patient by the name of Doctor Askin. He wouldn't
be with you, would he?"

"No, I am in Jennings, Oklahoma, at the present
time. How long has he been gone?"

"Mr. Feather, we checked in on the doctor last
night at bed check. He was not in the institution this
morning for breakfast. His bed has been slept in, but
we can't find him. A window has been jimmied from
the inside, and his overnight bag is missing. We knew
he was working on a project for you and all his pictures
from that project are gone, and we thought maybe he
was with you."

"Doctor Askin has not been working for me for some months now. As for the pictures, what did they look like?"

"We couldn't make hide nor hair of the scribbles on the rocks. It was as if Doctor Askin couldn't get the idea out of his head. He seems to be satisfied working on his old puzzles, and we left him alone most of the time. This project was different. There seemed to be an urgency behind him. Your name was on all the pictures along with Yonder Rock Project, dated several months ago. Doctor Askin is a ward of this institution, and we handle all his monetary finances. As far as we know, Doctor Askin doesn't have any money on him. We don't think he has any resources of any kind. If you do find him, please call us immediately."

"Miss Servers, we are headed back to my farm, and we will keep an eye out for him. If he shows up, please call me."

Little Bird and I motored back to the farm, and wouldn't you know it, the good Doctor Askin was in Sam's old teepee, passed out dead dog drunk! I ventured into the hide structure and salvaged the overfilled case of cave pictures, poured out all the shine, refilled the quart jars with water, tied the door shut, and let the old boy enjoy his misery. I figured the doctor had gotten enough money to buy out the supplies of the local moonshine still and had tied on a drunk that would have lasted several days had we not found the sot.

Little Bird and I set up camp with the motor home and tried to catch up on our sleep when Doctor Askin started his tirade trying to get out of the teepee. We gave him food and water the first day, and his cry went unheeded until we were good and ready to let him out. There is something about withdrawal symptoms that would just set me off. I had seen Sam so drunk from that moonshine, I guess I didn't care; I'd let him suffer.

I called the rehabilitation center, told them I would keep the doctor for a few days, and they in turn said they would come get him when I was through. You know, a few days in the drunk tank (teepee) settled the old boy down to making good sense. We walked to the Cimarron River, and he took a nice, sun-warmed bath. A good breakfast of countless pancakes and strong coffee made our live-in teepee guest much better to talk to.

"Mr. Chief Feather, you are the meanest man on the face of the earth, making me stay in that hot teepee."

"Yes, I am and will be the meanest man alive as long as you act like that. Now doctor, where did you get the money to travel?"

"You will not believe what I have found in the hieroglyphics!"

"Don't try to change the subject. First things first: where did you get the money?"

"It's a long story."

"Doctor, *where?*"

Silence! I thought, *I will get my answer first.*

"Okay, you are a hard man to ignore. All this goes back to the first time I was caught drinking too much. I was also a thief; I would steal from my fellow man as long as I could get all the whiskey that I wanted. All the time I worked for you I was watched like a hawk. That Doctor Brithen would not let me out of his sight. I found one of your lead marbles, hid it until last week, sold it to a guard, took the money, and helped myself to one good, stiff drink. Chief, you know the rest. I couldn't stop with one drink, and when you found me in that teepee, that was where I was going, to be a stiff.

I didn't care if Doctor Brithen was going to get me ready for my last box, I was going out drunk. You and Little Bird found me under the worst circumstances that befall a man caught in the act. Now, call the boys in the white coats to come get me. I guess I'm fired!"

"Nope. You are going to live in that teepee until you have learned your lesson. You go to the river to take a bath, drink the water that comes out of the spring, and catch your food just like my ancestors learned to do on this very land. I dare say in a month's time you will not be as fat as you are right now. I want you to take these pictures and figure out the secrets that befall this hillside. Little Bird and I will be in and out to check on you."

I got myself out of his sight before I laughed in his face. Mad?—you bet!—that a educated man like that could be caught up with drink and ruin his life. Little Bird and I kept up our anger, and I was surprised at the resilient old man. He found the hill spring, made a throwing stick to kill game, built up the cooking hearth in the teepee, and found all the wood to cook and keep warm by. I became proud when I saw a fresh-killed rabbit roasting on his spit. True to his instructions, he got all the hieroglyphics in the teepee and started his search. By the end of two weeks, we had a slimmer old man standing proud to be alive.

We heard him banging on our motor home and saying that he had figured out the pictures. Hieroglyphics were pictured wrong on the cave walls. Doctor Askin pointed out that the scenes were cut in the stone from right to left; whoever chiseled the hieroglyphics must have been left-handed. The pictures were set up in the teepee in a circle and showed a scrambled view. We looked until Little Bird exclaimed, "I found a scene from the hill side of Yonder Rock." Doctor Askin moved the respective photos, and we were standing in the middle of the Cimarron River looking up and over the banks at a herd of buffalo around Yonder Rock.

"Ah, we have the Rosetta Stone of the cave paleographic," said the sober doctor.

"Doctor Askin, speak English," spoke Little Bird.

"Oh, excuse me," mumbled Doctor Askin. "Paleographic is the study of ancient writings and pictographs. This is by far the most complete and perfect display of ancient art that I have ever seen. Since we have found the view of Yonder Rock, we should be able to find the upper chamber entrance. That view has been obliterated in time and erosion. Let's place other pictures around in a circle, and we should be able to gain some insight of the sculpture's vision."

Again, Little Bird took the advantage as she started her "Oh, oh!" Doctor Askin and I helped the lady arrange the pictures, and an all-new landscape appeared.

"Hmmm," came from deep in the Doctor's chest. "Yes, this is the upper entrance as it appeared in the past. See the pile of crystalline rocks on the top of the ground? When we excavated around the wagon, this had sunk in the hillside by at least twenty feet. This region is sure unstable. Let's go up on the hillside with these pictures, and I will show you the difference."

The Hummer made fast work of the trip, and we sat in the warm sunshine. As each picture came up, Doctor Askin explained the typography. "This section was the entrance to acres of caves with very unstable roofs of sandstone. The weathering of sandstone produces copious amounts of sand, hence the thick layer that we see in the landscape. When you and Little Bird were caught in the rock slide, was there a lot of dust?"

"We were in a continuous storm of flying sand. We were almost covered up with the storm, noise, and rock flying."

"You were very fortunate to escape from those circumstances. I don't know of any way to protect yourself from the flying sand and rocks. This is what is called compression; the rocks are being jammed together. Usually they compress and spring back, and then you have decompression and the falling away of the upper roof areas. Look at this set of pictures. The upper cave entrance is level with the ground on the other side of the hill. Now look at today's sunken entrance, and I estimate a twenty-foot depression. I have estimated that these pictographs are about twenty-five hundred to three thousand years old. How many depressions we have had in that length of time is anybody's guess. We could have another series of expansion and decompression at any time or could wait for another few millennia. Who knows?"

"Doctor Askin, I have really enjoyed the day with you, explaining away some the mysteries of Yonder Rock. Let's go to town and get a bucket of chicken and have a picnic down on the river."

"You know, Mr. Chief Feather, there are some of your aboriginal customs that really appeal to me. Maybe we can test my resolve and drive by some of the beer joints that used to appeal to my taste. Oh, and you probably *should* call the Alcohol Rehabilitation Center and have them send the boys in white coats for me. I might be missing some of those childish games they play, you know, like poker, blackjack, sewing, cooking. There's always something to stimulate the mind."

Miner's Legacy

The mystery of my great-great-grandfather Miner Feather left me with the feeling of incompleteness. I had been involved for more that a year trying to unravel the mystery of how he got two tons of gold made into gold-lead ingots. Yes, I had the molds marked "MF." His mark on each of the lead marbles came to light when Doctor Askin found a hairline crack that marked each marble. There was no doubt that Miner had molded each marble with his own hands. I got out the old ledger and reread all of Miner's notes. Little Bird would look over my shoulder, and we scoured each page for any clue to our history. On one of our nightly sessions, we discovered the first pages were smudged, dirty, and had previous usage. Every time we opened the journal, here were these dirty pages, and so help us, it never registered there might be a message there. My sweet wife, Little Bird, had the idea first from looking over my shoulder. There were words embossed under all the grime. By holding the light just right, we could see more writing. We knew we needed more help than we had. *Doctor Askin!*

An early morning call brought news that we didn't want to hear. The Alcohol and Rehabilitation ward had buried the doctor last week in the pauper's end of their graveyard. There was no family to claim the body, and since he was a ward of the state, he was interred immediately after death. Little Bird and I wished we could have done more but accepted his fate.

Doctor Brithen! But there was nothing, no trace, no phone. Boy this was getting old.

General Lance! General Lance was out of the states on assignment, so Little Bird and I were on our own again. A visit to the local police department gave us a lead to bring the complete, embossed script to light. A simple black light exposed the script of the journal, and we had another message to trace. The written language looked somewhat familiar to me; I just couldn't get the idea out of my head that I had seen the long flowing words before.

"Lone, the script is written in the Cherokee language," said Little Bird. "Look at the syllabify. It's the aboriginal language of our ancestors that lived in Georgia. Lone, we need to be careful who we show these notes to. They may contain information about where Miner got his gold."

I scanned the pages with the black light, and the following came through the dirt of two hundred years, all written in precise longhand with a feather quill and black ink. Little Bird and I could just stand and stare at our legacy. Little Bird started immediately with the translation. "This is the Universal Declaration of Human Rights, written by George Guess."

Nigada aniyvwi nigeguda'lvna ale unihloyi unadehna duyukdv gesv'l. Gejinela unadanvthdi ale unohisdi ale sagwu gesv junilvwisdanedi anahidinvdlv anahidin vdlv adanvdo gvhdi. George Guess

Little Bird and I stood glaring at our legacy coming from the written language of Cherokee, called Tsaliagi. Her translation was written in small delicate rounded letters.

> All human beings are born free and equal in dignity and rights. They are endowed with reason and conscience, and should act towards one another in a spirit of brotherhood.

> Signed by George Guess,
> Chief Sequoyah of the Cherokee 1808

"Lone, you don't suppose this is an original document?"

"I don't know."

"This document shows the Declaration was written years before it was published in 1819. This could upset the actual dates."

"Would this document change history one iota?"

"No. In fact, since this is a copy of a copy, there could be a big-to-do over nothing."

"Okay, for the time being let's translate the complete text, and we will keep a lid on our findings."

Diary of Woodrow P. Olson

3 September 1808: made a note to finalize the draft of syllabify.

18 September 1808: Chief Sequoyah gave me rough drafts of his Cherokee syllabify to edit. I looked it over and made a couple of notes and sent it back as is.

20 September 1808: News came that the United States was going to relocate all Cherokee Indians to Indian Territory.

24 January 1809: The news is terrible. Our people started rioting against the government and are being forced to start to Indian Territory on foot without any provisions.

20 Feburary 1809: I was asked to accompany a contingent of Cherokee leaders as a scribe into Indian Territory.

1 April 1809: Met with the leaders of the trail committee to form a traveling government for the arduous journey into Indian Territory.

9 May 1809: Another meeting with the trail committee. Nothing was decided.

7 August 1809: Money was set aside to buy all new equipment, young horses, guides, and take as much money as we could.

3 October 1809: Made application to the United States government for safe travel to the unknown Indian Territories.

14 December 1809: Was notified to meet with the representative of the United States government to finalize the trail permit to Indian Territories.

7 January 1810: The meeting was held in the offices of the Cherokee Nation. This turned out to be the worst day of my life. All the officers of the trail committee were arrested by the militia. All funds were attached, the offices were declared meeting places of the terrorists; all the families were rounded up without notice or provisions. The drive west was started tonight as we were ushered out into the night air without coats or boots of any kind.

8 January 1810: I did have my riding boots on and was able to walk along with the group of maybe fifty travelers going west. We were made to walk all the next night, and I felt if I could hide out in the woods, I could get back to some of my relations named Feather. As luck would have it, I wore black clothing and the first ditch that I could hide in received my bulk. There were others that had the same idea, and we kept separate so as not to bring attention. The parade of Indians going west seemed endless. I hid in an old dugout the first day and walked the next night back to Walnut Grove, Georgia.

I hid in an old lead mine until a young man discovered me. He grabbed a shovel and would have caved my head in until I pled for mercy. "Please don't hit me. Please!"

A grown man spoke. "What you want here?" came from under his big floppy hat.

"The militia, the army wants to send me to Indian Territory, and I can't walk that far; I will die."

"From the looks of the fat on you, I think you could walk that far. Get out of here!"

"Okay, but don't hit me with that shovel. Oh, you wouldn't know where the Feather clan lives, would you?"

This stopped the challenge with, "What is your name, fellow?"

"My name is Dr. Woodrow P. Olson. I'm a linguistic professor for the college at Atlanta, Georgia."

"Well, hello there, Woody. I'm Miner Feather. You must be our mother's brother. Sara and I have wondered where you got off to."

"Miner, you would not believe what has happened. We have been trying to reason with the United States Government. Ever since the government bought the Louisiana Purchase in 1803 they have got it in their heads to move all Indians to Indian Territory out west. Our contingent of Cherokee leaders has tried establishing a government to rule ourselves. We have been picked up and forced to walk to this area called Indian Territory in the center of the purchase. We had no provisions of any kind. I escaped and walked back to Walnut Grove and am hiding out in this mine. Miner, I'm too old and fat to walk that far, and beside that it's in the wintertime. I might freeze."

"Yes, Woody, it's a long way to where they want us to go. Tell you what, you stay in this lead mine, and I will see what I can do. I will bring you food and water if you will give your word to not be moving around the countryside where the militia can see you."

"I will do anything you say. Just don't let them find me. By the way, how is my niece Sara—is she alright?"

"Yes, Sara is ok. I will get back home, and we will figure something out."

Miner left me for the night and I got caught up on my sleep. I ate his sandwich in one mouth full, wished for more, but I kept my word and stayed in the mine. Sara and Miner came sometime in the night and brought me some more water. We talked into the wee hours, and I asked Sara to go fix me a big bacon and egg sandwich. "Nope" came from my niece. She said that the Militia was looking for a big, fat politician. She was going to do something about all that flab, and maybe just maybe they could hid me. I should have caught on there that they were going to starve me to death!

Miner came the next day, and we talked about what I had been doing for all these years.

"I have been working on the Cherokee language and how it was such a mess to understand."

"Is that why I can't understand some of my relations, Woody?"

"Exactly. I have a Cherokee alphabet almost ready to write on paper, and I speak all the known Cherokee Indian dialects to date." I paused after my explanation. A question was weighing on me and had been for some time.

"Miner, what is going to happen, we can't live like this forever?"

"Don't ask questions!"

9 January 1810: I've had another bad day but did get a small portion to eat and a large amount to think about. I had made a major blunder, and time will tell

PAT LORETT

if we will have to pay for this. My ornery relation is bent on starving me to death, and that little ole man is the boss of the whole clan. Sara sent me a change of cloths that was way too tight and not near enough food, but plenty of water. I will show them. I'll not complain and take life as it comes along. They burned my city clothes and made me wear the undersize until I stunk like work!

12 January 1810: I finally got caught up on my sleep and discovered I could bend over much better. My shoes aren't near as tight; Miner came in during the night and told me that I had to be out of the mine by daylight tomorrow. He came with a light and led me to their house in the dark. We turned around several times, and I wound up on the back step with coffee in my hand. Miner left and was gone a few minutes when the ground trembled, the house shook, the trees swayed, and all I could think was *earthquake*.

As Miner returned, Sara said, "Is it done?"

"Yep, we can leave now."

"What happened?" I asked.

"Woody, you promised to not ask questions; now quit."

Made me so mad I thought about pouting, but soon got over that with another cup of coffee. "Sara, your house sure smells good and homely. Could you fix me some bacon and eggs and maybe some of your good bread?" Sara looked right at me, and I knew then I wasn't going to get any bacon and eggs. "Nope." That was all that I got!

13 January 1810: I helped hook up two teams onto a loaded Conestoga wagon. We tied a milk cow to the wagon and got on the trail in time to meet several other wagons, stock, more teams, people, and several small

kids. Nobody ever said a word, but I could feel we were headed to Indian Territory! I was told to not say a word of English to anybody; the language was switched to a Cherokee dialect that I had never heard before. Miner drove his wagon with Sara riding in another wagon, and I had to walk behind the milk cow. I thought, *maybe they will switch off with me cause I'm an old man, and I'm fat and I can't walk very far.* We didn't stop for dinner, and I only got my bread and water. Dark came ever so slowly, and I piled up under the wagon and tried to sleep. Between the bugs, cows, mules, horses, and dogs, sleep didn't come very quick.

14 January 1810: Miner's long ear'd donkey woke us. I hurt all over. There was not one place that felt normal. I noticed that my clothes were loose all over. I gulped my bread and a gallon of water, and they pointed me down the trail. By the end of the second day, Miner said we were ten miles down the trail and not making good time. I thought, *I hope that runt falls off his wagon and breaks his neck.* Then I thought about him being the leader, and that made me mad. All this madness made me sleep the sleep of the dead the second night.

15 January 1810: I must have not moved or twitched until that donkey woke the dead the next morning. I thought that I was dead, then I thought, *dead men don't hurt.* I don't know when we started seeing all kinds of human skeletons beside the trail. Our doctor told us not to handle any human remains; that was a sure call for blood-borne diseases. That wake-up call put shivers up and down my slimmer build.

16 January 1810: The Tennessee River hovered in the distance. I don't know what I was thinking, but swimming was not on my agenda. I complained to the leader (Miner), and he just shrugged his shoulders

and said, "Sink or swim." As his wagon slowly sank, I was holding onto the back gate, and I sank too. I felt a rope circle my middle, and whoever drug me across the river was not gentle to say the least. There must have been a dozen ropes used to pull that Conestoga across the river, of all the whooping and hollering at such a feat. Miner got wet but managed the traverse very well. There was a lot of discussion about his wagon not floating, and it was decided it needed to be dried out and animal fat slathered on the seams. Can you imagine who got picked to apply real fat on that wagon? The day came when the wagon was proclaimed dry, and the voice came on the wind. "Woody, let's you and me waterproof my wagon so it will float!" You guessed it; I was first in line with a bucketful of rancid grease and rags. The thing that really amazed me was that Miner could stand up under his wagon and out work any two men. The job didn't take long, but the clean up was not to be. Miner spoke so officially: "Woody, let's not take a bath until we're in Indian Territory. Maybe the militia won't bother us!" I worried myself sick about that statement—not enough to miss my bread and water, but I did grumble at my plight.

"Woody, I see that you are writing the day-by-day accounts of this trip, and in a way, that's good. I want you to write so nobody can understand. What do you recommend?"

"I'm writing all this in the Cherokee dialect that you are speaking. There is not a white man alive, much less a Cherokee, that will understand it."

"I will have to trust you with that responsibility and thank you for coming with us."

My spirits were lifted; I had something to do except walk along behind and lose weight.

17 January 1810: Long Ears woke us in the night got the dogs to barking, and I was afraid of the dark. I heard a thunderous explosion above the wagon and screeching cries in the night. All I could do was hide my ears and pray that I didn't get shot or scalped. The noise subsided and the word was out—men had gotten killed. I couldn't help but look, and there was blood all over the ground. This made me sick, and I lost all my bread and water from the last week. Miner was a model of command. He instructed graves dug, white bodies stacked like cord wood, horses stripped bare, then turned loose with our herd.

Then all six white raiders were buried in one grave. Brush was used to dust out all signs of blood. I had gotten over being sick and helped where I could. The hardest part was taking hold of a dead man; I had to take another turn losing my meals. Miner came by and spoke the words that I will remember forever.

"Straighten up there, Woody, you can be sick after we get on the trail!"

Every man, woman, and child helped get us going in the middle of the night. We left all the evidence in the back woods and hoped for the best.

18 January 1810: We traveled in the back woods of Georgia that I had never seen. The outriders came in with a fresh-killed deer that they hung on the back of Miner's wagon. I told Miner that I could never eat anything that had blood on it. Miner's response is something I want to write down for the ages to come.

"That's fine with me, but we are out of bread and the water is getting scarce. If you want to lose more weight than what you have, just don't take any of our stick-roasted deer meat tonight."

I thought on the matter and decided right then that I was a full-blooded Cherokee Indian and could eat like my ancestors did. Ahhh, I've made that decision— okay, on with the trailing. Imagine this: the field-dressed deer swinging on the tailgate, dripping blood. Indian kids coming with a knife, cutting the fat out and leaving with a mouthful. I tried to gag but did hold it down. Then the idea came into my head that I could do the same thing as those kids. My body was craving anything I could get down my throat. The first mouthful of raw deer meat must have grown in size, and yes, I lost part of it. The second tasted better, and Miner interjected this:

"Woody, if I was you, I would go slowly on that raw deer."

I didn't, and you know what happened next. I was glad a hungry dog came by and ate my mess!

The clan camped by a small stream for the night and built a good cooking fire. The deer was cut into small strips and roasted, and we ate all we could hold and gave the rest to the Indians on the trail. There seemed an endless line to snatch a stick of roasted deer and then shuffle off down the trail.

19 January 1810: I kind of got into a daze walking along behind in the dust. If the wagon stopped, I stopped. Such was the sight one day when the militia came by.

"Halt, don't go any further. We're looking for a Dr. Woodrow P. Olson from the University of Atlanta, Georgia." Miner just sat on the wagon seat with his blank expression like he didn't understand a word. One of our elders came and signed for them to let us alone. The sergeant said again that they were looking for the terrorist Dr. Woodrow P. Olson. The elder signed for them to leave us alone. I could hear the soldiers talking amongst themselves.

"Let's search this wagon; he has got to be here somewhere." The wind switched about this time, and all the militia could smell was rotting meat fat, hot sweaty bodies, horse, donkey, and smelly dogs. The soldiers fell back and had second thoughts about a close search. Another word came from the sergeant: "Men, this group looks okay. Let's travel on down the line."

The elder gave the sign, and we ambled on over the hill with not a smile on our faces. I knew then I was all wrong about this clan, that Miner Feather just might pull this caper off. We held our peace until after dark and had to hold each other up from the laugh we had. I can't remember what we had for supper, but everybody came by and thanked me for holding my tongue.

Miner came and squinted his beady eyes at me and said, "Dr. Woodrow P. Olson—is that your full name?"

"Yes, that is the name on my graduation papers from the University of Atlanta, Georgia. That age is over now; I consider it an honor to be called Woody from this day hence. I suppose where we're going, that degree will not be worth the paper it's written on."

"Yes Woody, we're headed to a wild, untamed land to start all over with life. Are you up to the challenge?"

"Miner, as of two weeks ago, I was as a whimpering child not getting my way, not getting enough fattening food, having to sleep with the dogs and, by the way, that spotted one is the warmest. Miner, do you have any idea where we are going to settle?"

"All I have is the map of the Louisiana Purchase with the major rivers marked. When we get into Indian Territory, all this clan will most likely split up into the different families. You pick out where you want to go, we'll shake hands, and part. We have a long way to go yet, and let's make plans as we go. I'm sure the Lord will help us plan."

"Yes, the best plan is to go forth in the Lord's name."

20 January 1810: I had tried to make plans for almost two years, and all I did was wonder. Nothing happened in that bureaucratic atmosphere. We had been on the trail for two weeks and gotten further then ever before. Our day-to-day existence was just that, day by day, trying to travel further away from the troubled lands. Miner called an evening meeting, and we all sat around the fires trying to catch each word. He told about us getting to the Mississippi River and what he expected. He again warned us not to talk to anyone and let the elders do the signing.

21 January 1810: We felt the Mississippi long before it hove into view, and we could hardly see the west side. I had started to rely on our leaders, and that was the best for me. Our elder made a deal to have a flat-bottom barge take our whole clan over in one load for two horses. As it turned out, the barge owner got two of the outlaw's horses that had filled up on the grass along the trail. I wondered then if we would spend the other four on boat transport before we got into Indian Territory. How I could hold my peace was a wonder. I could have said a lot and spoiled the deal, but no, I kept my mouth shut and laughed within. Miner never said a word as he led us over the next hill before we congratulated each other.

6 February 1810: After a month on the trail, I realized I was going to live. My baggy pants hung on me like a tent and we were making much better time. As we started into Arkansas, the land turned out to be

rocks of all sizes, all made to punish the human body. Why the United States wanted the Louisiana Purchase was a mystery. I finally realized that Indian Territory was situated in the very center, and they needed a place to send all the unwanted Indians to get them out of the way. Well, so be it, all my education as a linguist was for naught, and I would be useless in the territories. Miner always sat in his wagon seat and usually chided me for walking so slow.

"Wake up there, Dr. Professor Woodrow P. Olson. I want to talk, come ride on my seat for a spell." I tried to climb, but I still had way too much backing there somewhere.

"Whoa, stop Woody, you about turned the wagon over!" We had a good laugh about me wallowing around on the ground. This was the turning point in my relationship with Miner Feather.

"What does it take to become a linguist?

"Linguistics is the study of languages, dialects, why they change and into what."

"Okay, Woody, that is the answer that I wanted. Is that why the Cherokee language is such a mess? We can't understand each other's family if they live someplace else?"

"Exactly. Your grandfather spoke differently than you and we are left with the mess of translations. Before the deportation of the Cherokee tribes and clans were started by the United States government, that was my job—trying to translate all the different dialects into one central language. I had been working with George Guess on this very problem, and we were close to having a Cherokee alphabet completed."

"Can you remember the alphabet?"

"I have the alphabet memorized and am ready to convert this into the written word."

"If I was to get you paper, quills, and black ink, could you write all this?"

"If you can get these supplies, I will teach you how to write the alphabet."

"Okay, a deal is a deal. While we are on the trail, you try to write whenever we are stopped. Let me see what I can come up with in supplies while you sharpen your memory."

"If you start to learn the Cherokee alphabet, you will have it down pat before we get into Indian Territory."

LEGAL SCHOLARS

I, Miner Feather, started this day in March 1810 to write the day journal of Indian Territory. Doctor Woodrow P. Olson became my teacher and mentor. I didn't tell him that I had talked to our lawyer, Sam Rignor, and found all the supplies we would ever need to write the Cherokee Alphabet. I felt a deal was a deal, and Woody kept his end of the bargain. Woody was a sharp teacher. He only gave me a few letters at a time and let me learn at my own speed.

I spoke with our lawyer, Sam, and wanted a paper that would let us own land in Indian Territory so nobody could steal it out from under us.

"Miner, there is no government in Indian Territory. I will have to go the Bureau of Indian Affairs to get a land patent submitted in your name. That document will have to be written in Cherokee and English before we settle into the territories."

"Sam, I know the perfect person to get all that done. You start the papers and I'll get you two together so our whole Feather clan will be protected." And off I went to find Woody.

"Woody, oh Woody, I have a perfect job for you."

"Miner, I've learned to avoid your offers. What is on your mind?"

I got those two scholars together, and the last I saw was them hunched over the documents that would last for ages to come, saying something that sounded like "land patent for ole short stuff."

Arkansas was almost the graveyard for all the Feather clan. Smallpox ravaged the land for weeks on end. We lost two squaws and one child, which would have left us unable to travel on, but travel we did for fear of the militia. We needn't have worried; they feared the smallpox too. Our doctor wrote "smallpox" on the sides of our wagons, and people steered clear of our stinking mess.

There was a mystery about our milk cow and small-pox that was never solved. Francy, as she was known, was tied to the back of my wagon and walked with Woody all day everyday. My entourage consisted of the kids, L'ear, Woody, and anybody that wanted a ride or wanted milk. Francy could be milked anywhere or any-time, so we turned Francy loose at night to forage with the other animals. By the next morning, she was bel-lowing her head off to be milked. Herein lies the mys-tery: anybody that drank the milk, was around Francy, or had any contact with her didn't have the smallpox as bad. In fact, Woody didn't have the smallpox at all. He milked her and fed the raw milk to anybody that could sit up and drink. Even anybody that ate the butter was protected. I talked to the doctor about this anomaly and his stoic answer was "Nope." Oh well, doctors have been known to be wrong sometimes.

During the smallpox scourge, I found the love of my life from a wagonload of diseased and dead Indians. Her name turned out to be Nell, and she had two small boys. I took charge of Orville, her brother that had never spoke, and helped them back to health. Nell's husband had died on the trail and the family was destitute. My heart was broken at seeing the plight. We gathered the elders, and Nell and I stepped across a bow and we became man and wife while on the trail to our destiny.

We approached the Indian Territory line and never knew where we were. We finally figured out the militia knew and left us to our land. It was as if a weight had been lifted off our lives and the real test began. We were out of food, water, supplies, our stock were poor, and we were dirty. I called a clan meeting, and we decided to spend the winter of 1810 recharging our lives beside the Illinois River. Our first bath of months of trail riding got the lice off our bodies. We washed our hair and discovered that all of us were bone thin, including Dr. Woodrow P. Olson. He didn't even look like the same man; no, he was not the same. His spirit became true Cherokee Indian, and his work took on an all new vision. I don't know who caught the first fish, but we all fattened up on fried fish, baked fish, raw fish, dried fish—you name it, we fixed a royal buffet. Throngs of Indians came by and never knew what they ate—it was cooked, and that was all that mattered.

By the springtime of 1811 our doctor, lawyer, and linguist had worked many a day writing the land patents. The presentations were given out to each family head with instructions to use them when claiming the

Indian Territory lands. If these patents were not used, the land could be taken without their permission.

Our trail ride ended in Indian Territory as we split up with that handshake. I wondered then if we would ever see each other again. Miner Feather, 1811.

Little Bird and I were amazed at what had been derived from the journal. We got out the original land patent of Miner Feather and saw the signatures of: Miner Feather, owner; Nell Feather, wife; Dr. Sam Rignor, lawyer; Dr. Woodrow P. Olson, linguist; Dr. George Hunt, witness.

The rest of Miner's journal was about after they had moved on to the Cimarron River section of land, his discovery of Yonder Rock, and moving the lead-covered gold ingots into the hiding place of the age. All of these entries were erased until Little Bird took the black light and his old script leapt into the twenty-first century. Our lives were humbled at the greatness of these men and women that sacrificed to ensure the Indian Nations a land of salvation.

Little Bird and I considered our lot and resolved ourselves to serving the Lord and helping our fellow tribesmen.

One last note: We were the picture of health, but that ole morning sickness came every morning and hung on her shoulders. Even I had sympathy pains, and we took turns hanging over the rail fence. Bad? *Nawww*, it was our turn to add to the Feather clans.

BUBBA'S FISHIN'

Little Bird and I had our noses to the written pages of history much too long. We decided to head to Mannford and look up Bubba and the fishermen. We found Nell and Pell beside themselves. Bubba and their husbands had gone on one of their fishing forays up the Cimarron River and hadn't come back. It had been two days now, and they hadn't taken any food. I knew just where those fishermen were; a quick trip to the boathouse got me an airboat completely outfitted and a full scuba tank. I droned to the old home place in less than an hour. Little Bird had stayed with the twins to man the telephone, and I took my cell just in case. I soon found the twins on a sandbar, but no Bubba. Of course, the twins spoke at the same time, and finally I got the word that Bubba had swum under a rock ledge and hadn't come out. I let caution prevail and remember how that flathead had scratched my arm in his mouth. A wet suit, tanks, gloves, and a waterproof flash light put me under the rock ledge on the trail of fisherman Bubba.

Folks, if you have never been in a flathead's lair before, let me caution you—that thing will attack you with the ferocity of a lion. This was no exception. His first lunges got my thigh, arm, back, the air tank and carried me back out into the river. I stood up in the shallow water and the twins helped me out onto the sandbar.

"Chief, we heard the fracas, but we was afeared to come any closer—that thang is mean! We heard Bubba back in them rocks somewhere. He's alive!"

"Boys, that fish is bound and determined to run me off. What do you recommend?"

The twin husbands said as one, "We know what to do, but we'ss scared to take the bait in under the rocks—we'ss afeared that thang will drown us in the deep water."

"Show me, and maybe we can catch us a good 'un."

The answer came wrapped in a gunnysack with a long, stout rope connected to the eyelet. I felt the sack and discovered a treble hook the size of a hay hook. Let me tell you, it didn't take me long to understand where to carry this. I got my scuba gear straightened out and back I went in the lair again, trailing the rope. I can't describe the feeling when that flathead grabbed the sack and was hooked good and deep. All I wanted to do was get out of the way. The twins both drug 104 pounds of very mad catfish out of his hole. I turned on the flashlight and found a very scared Bubba about ready to try to dig through rock to get out of the underwater cave.

"Oh Chief, I just knew you would come get me. That fish has had me treed for two days and now we lost 'em."

We shared my scuba tank and swam out from under the rock ledge in time to see the twins drag Mr. Flathead out on the sandbar. Bubba couldn't believe we had the fish, and all he could do was start blubbering, his eyes red. Just as quickly, Bubba dried his eyes and said, "Boys, there is another in there. Let's do it again."

"No!" all of us chimed in. "Enough is enough. Let's go home."

We motored home in time to have a king-sized fish fry that evening, much to the delight of the women folks. We told lies until we couldn't and slept the sleep of hard-working men. I tried to give Bubba his lead marbles, and he again said that they weren't no good.

"In fact, let's go out to the boat shed. I want to show you something. Chief, I want to be completely honest with you. I think you are not understanding what I'm saying about them marbles not being no good. I discovered two years ago that the inside of the marbles was gold. I never told my family about what they were worth or nuttin'. My family can't handle money in any way. All the twins like to do is drink up their paychecks until they are drunk skunks. I decided then to never tell them what we had, and that seems to be the very thing to do. Keeping them broke and going fishing is the very best.

"Chief, I want you to give all that money away and never say where it came from. You and Little Bird seem to be able to handle money, and I want you to have that control."

I had found another man that could handle the trials of life. Little Bird and I took our motor home and yellow Hummer and got on the road of finding more of Miner's legacy.

CHEROKEE STRIP

We got back on the road with our camping style. We loved outdoor living as long as the Winnebago or Hummer took us there. Little Bird coined the phrase "spoiled rotten Indians living off the land."

I came back with, "Yes, as long as we have fast food—you know, golden arches, the king, soup in a bread shell, and relations that would feed everybody that was in the yard come meal time." Our all-time favorite became food with company!

We had not been northwest. I put the sun on our windshield and made Kay County before dark. An overnight stay at the Wal-Mart parking lot with several other campers put us at the museum for opening bell. We walked the outside walking trail until my sweet wife said, "That's enough of that." I hadn't noticed her pink face in the fresh morning air and her sweet breath making a fog.

We tied our sweaters around our middles and got warm inside the museum. We had learned to look for those gold-lead marbles. A sudden intake of air from Little Bird pointed out three of the telltale fifty-caliber balls. We looked them all over and read the inscription:

> The above picture is an original copy of a tin-type taken while the Chisholm Trail was on the east side of I-35. This person is three foot eleven, a full-grown Cherokee Indian known as Trader Joe. Trader Joe gave the trail boss these lead balls as payment for cattle lost to the Indian Nations. If there is anybody out there who knows anything to add to this, please contact the director.

Little Bird and I decided it was coffee time and retired to our motor home!

"Is there no end to Miner's contribution to the Indian Nations?" asked Little Bird.

"I hope there isn't. His original theme lives on today within us. It's too late to travel home today. How about some Chinese food? We'll stay at Wal-mart and head in after breakfast tomorrow."

"Sounds good to me. I'm tired already." I put Little Bird to bed early and cruised the TV channels. The first news was an APB for a couple wanted for income tax evasion, theft of Indian artifacts, flight to avoid prosecution, etc. I thumbed them off and joined my sleeping wife. I never thought much about the news of the day, but I couldn't get the museum story off my mind and rolled around all night and woke at daylight the next morning. Little Bird finally came out, stretching her style, and wanted a cup of hot coffee. Absentmindedly,

PAT LORETT

I hit the TV button and found the same news about the wanted couple. They had been located with twenty pounds of lead marbles and an old tintype. My great-great-grandfather Miner Feather was on TV! I jotted the phone number down and grabbed my cell phone.

If anybody had got in our way to the police department, they would have been trampled. A sergeant invited us to an interrogation room, and our taped interview went as follows.

"Good morning, Lone Feather. My name is Sergeant Jim Ames, and this is my partner, Sergeant Pattie Hoyle. You said in our phone conversation that you had other evidence pertaining to the museum theft. At the present time, we have to withhold the names of the accused for their protection, but we can advance the investigation. Lone and Little Bird, what is your connection with this case?"

"Sergeant, you displayed a picture of my great-great grandfather Miner Feather. We had been out to the museum yesterday and saw the same picture in a display case. The note in the case wanted more information, and we decided to decline at that time."

"What makes you think that the picture we displayed on the TV was your grandfather?" I opened my briefcase and pulled out an eight-by-eleven glossy of Miner Feather and gave them the picture. It was an exact match except mine was in color. A door opened, and a caseworker came in and whispered to Sergeant Ames. His nod brought the report that the couple had bonded out and were ready to leave. The sergeant turned to me and asked if I had any more evidence to present at this time.

"We have lots more evidence to present, including proof that the marbles were the same ones from the museum and that they were connected to the family estate of Miner Feather."

We heard a fracas start out in the hallway. Both sergeants said, "Please excuse us" and hurried to the sounds. Little Bird and I could only imagine the ruse that developed. We bided our time, and the sergeants returned, ruffled but intact.

"Sergeant Hoyle, separate those two. We may have an ironclad case of grand theft here."

"I'm sorry for the interruption. Let's proceed; the recorder is still running. Now we have a picture of your grandfather in question. Do you have proof positive of that statement?"

"Yes, we have had a rather large estate question, and I have positive DNA tests proving that is my grandfather." I produced the documents signed by Doctor Brithin, witnessed by Doctor Askin, and dated. Sergeant Hoyle returned, nodding that all was done, and we got on with the interview.

"May I have permission to copy all of these documents? We will have to fax our departments to check these signatures."

"You can copy any of our documents as long as they are not out of our sight."

"We can do one thing better than that." A stenographer with all necessary equipment set up shop in interrogation room number two, and the wheels of progress started to hum.

"Okay, Lone, what is next? You said you had more?"

"The TV mentioned that twenty pounds of lead marbles had been found with the couple. Do you have them in the evidence locker?"

"Yes, all that evidence is locked up in our lockers under constant surveillance with an armed guard."

"Here is an analysis of the lead marbles that were in the estate of Miner Feather.

"You mean those lead marbles are really gold with a lead cover?"

"Yes, Sergeant, there were 216 troy ounces of gold in that bucket at today's price of a thousand dollars per ounce. You do the math."

I heard the wheels squeak and come up with $216,000 and a very audible sigh.

"Sergeant Ames, you need to have the lead marbles checked with your forensic laboratory, and I'm sure they will agree with these findings. We found a quick way to trace the journey of the marbles is with a black light. You will know immediately." Another quick call ensued and brought another department to arms.

"Little Bird and I were at the museum yesterday and found three lead marbles with the picture in question. They should be confiscated immediately; there might be a temptation to steal them too."

A phone call from some unknown party was answered by Sergeant Hoyle. "Yes, yes, okay. Test them while they are in the holding tank and call us with the results."

The hidden talk was dropped as Sergeant Hoyle reported that the black light tests were positive and the prisoners were going to get a quick test too. Fax reports poured into our cubicle that all our papers were in order. Another interruption brought the interview to a temporary end. Sergeant Ames explained the couple had requested a lawyer before any interview with them, and he wanted us to be behind the one-way glass to see if we had seen them before. I requested a recording of our conversation behind the glass, and we all filed into our seats.

As interrogations go, the man was ho-hum and never said too much. The woman filled us in with plenty. Her lawyer kept trying to shush the idle talk that was digging a hole of a jail term for years to come. I couldn't get the woman out of my mind until she turned sideways, and then I recognized her as the woman in the museum looking on with us. Our stenographer recorded all our conversations, and we met back with Sergeant Ames.

"Did this couple look familiar to you?"

"Yes, the woman was in the museum with us while we were looking at the lead marbles. We had not seen the man at any time."

"Okay, Chief Warrant Officer Lone Feather, you have passed all our examinations that we have thrown at you. We know that you have top-secret clearance from your service record. You are not to talk to anyone about this case until further notice. You have been known to us from the first time you pulled into the museum. Our cameras have recorded your every move.

"Now I would like to play the video of your Winnebago and show you what this couple has been doing." Little Bird and I sat spellbound as our life played out for the last forty-eight hours. The couple had been watching us because of the interest in the three lead marbles.

"Now, Lone and Little Bird, I need for you to listen to what I have to say. I'm sorry for the intrusion in your life, but I'm here to inform you that this investigation is on the FBI level. Sergeant Hoyle and I are federal agents. Please listen to this conversation and confirm that they are your voices."

It was as if a rerun was played of our voices when we came out of the museum, overnight in the Wal-Mart parking lot, even to the phone calls made to the police department. "Yes, Sergeant Ames, if that is your name, those are our voices. Now what else should we know?"

"Chief Lone Feather, the lead-gold marbles will be in legation for some time. Their disposal will be to the museums that file a loss."

"That is the purpose of the Miner Legacy. Little Bird and I are trying to further the work started by Miner."

"Okay, Chief, we have been investigating a string of robberies over the state of Oklahoma for some time, always the same thing. It seems this couple has been seen in each museum of the robberies in question. These lead marbles were the only items stolen and the picture of your relation this time. We don't know if they have been following you or they just travel in hopes of finding them and you happened to be here.

"We have made a connection to a former employee of the Alcohol and Rehabilitation ward in Shawnee Oklahoma. I believe this employee was a nephew of a Doctor Askin that worked with you on assignment of General Lance's investigation of Sam Feather. Doctor Askin made off with one of those lead marble and peddled it to the investigated subject of this investigation. We couldn't figure where Dr. Askin come up with so much money or where he spent it. That is a mystery in itself. We knew he spent some time with you, and all we found in his tent was water in a jar. His tent smelled of whiskey, but so help me there was not a drop but water in those jars. Do you suppose he drank up all that money he had?"

"Sergeant Ames, if I told you what was in those jars that smelled of whiskey, you wouldn't believe me it must have been a mistake of the FBI!"

"No, the FBI doesn't make mistakes. What is that mystery, off the record of course?"

"I don't believe the FBI is ever off record."

"Well okay, but we would like to tie all the loose ends. We want to thank you for your honesty and to shake your hand and thank you for serving in the Iraq and Kuwait theaters. Little Bird, we want to congratulate you on your coming child.

"Oh, and one more thing, Chief Feather." The two agent gave me a sharp salute.

Little Bird and I got in our Winnebago connected to our Hummer and motored on Highway 177 going south. We didn't say a word until we were almost to the Cimarron River.

"Lone, is there any thing that the FBI doesn't know?"

I looked each way and said "Shhhhh!"

Deep Fork

We set up camp on the ole home place and were ready to spend some quality time resting up. That last foray with the FBI left us weary of digging into our history, but foot—it was ours and we knew we would try again. I tried all the look-up history sites on the Internet: dnatribes. com, even searched some blogs. Little Bird did a cruise of Google Earth of the Creek Nations. She found Creek Indian Museum at Okmulgee. Well, what the heck? We might as well see what the Creek Nation was doing.

Dripping Springs S. P. had room for our motor home before dark, and we slept the clock around. Little Bird got back on the Net and was ready to close out when I heard her shout. "Oh Lone, come quick, I think I have found a wanted tracer on some of our relations! Look at this Web site." A picture had been posted that showed a short man that looked like Miner with a complete family. Miner was standing on the front row with his floppy hat, several kids and a woman that looked the same as him. All the children are in matching suits. No names, just a phone number and an inquiry for information about the pictures.

"Little Bird, be careful. That may be a scam. Let's do some investigating and see what we can find."

My detective work didn't turn up much except a name of Olson that lived in Depew by Interstate 44. We got out the map and decided to let that lead pass for the time being. An all-day trip to the Creek Indian Museum showed us a lot of Indian-looking people but no definite leads. We looked at every picture until we were blue in the face. I was glad to find an old friend for a take-out meal—you know, the king. Our evening turned out to be an old movie on the boob tube, sleep came slow, and I woke star-struck awake.

"Olson, Olson! Little Bird, wake up, that name I found while searching those phone records was a distant relation to Miner. You don't suppose that Miner had a second family in Creek County."

"Don't let your imagination run amuck. Miner was a fine Christian man, and all the records we have showed he was faithful to Nell all their married life."

"Don't let Miner fool you. Those traveling salesmen have a reputation, and things happen while on the road. All those kids sure look like Miner!"

We brought up the Web site again, and I printed all the pictures on glossy film paper. The more pictures we printed that morning, the more we thought about Miner Feather having a second family with six kids. I printed the last group pictures of the whole clan before we discovered the likeness of the woman. "Little Bird, this picture is a group setting of an all-together different family. Look at the mother; she is an exact image of Miner, and this has to be a sister. The large, heavy man in the background is most likely Woodrow P. Olson, her husband. Miner Feather is in his usual trail garb, with that big floppy hat."

"I can see it now. Miner is visiting the Olson clan; a tintype photographer came by and snapped history in the making. Lone, let's get back to sleep, and we will travel to Depew in the morning and try to find this clan."

Morning brought another of those Oklahoma high humidity days, and we enjoyed the back roads toward I-44. I answered the email request for information about the pictures and got an immediate answer from a W. P. Olson. "Lone Feather, we had about given up on finding anybody with the pictures. Do you have any tintypes about that era? Please call me on my cell, as I am out tending my girls."

We sat down in the trailer park, left the motor home, and scouted out the local phone directory for any Olsons. We found the W. P. Olson but that was all. A trip to the local co-op got me enough information to last a week. Seems that W. P. was a local cattleman and was running a cow-calf operation on the grasslands of Creek County, and if I would have a free cup of coffee, I would get to meet W. P. in just a few minutes. A very nice dully weighed across the scales, filled up with range cubes, the driver parked his cowboy Cadillac, and in strode a larger version of Miner Feather dressed in working cowboy garb with cow crap on his boots. W. P. signed the bill and poured himself a cup of coffee. By this time, I had my pictures laying on the table, and W. P., as he was called, came alive. All the old farmers got to see a real reunion of the descendants of the walk over from Walnut Grove, Georgia, in 1810.

"W.P Olson this is Little Bird, my wife, and my name is Lone Feather, Jr."

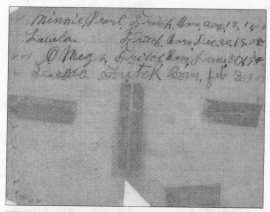

GETTING TOGETHER AGAIN

All we could do was hold each other and wonder what took so long to enjoy family again.

"Lone, you are a sight to see after wondering all these years where we came from, where we were going. Do you have any written records to tell about our grandfathers?"

"Yes, we have so many records that it will take us a lifetime to catch up. Is there any place we can meet and spread all these out to catch you up to the present times? These tintypes that are on this table are an exact match to the ones you have on the Internet. There is no doubt we are cousins five times over."

"Yes, I'm convinced we need to meet your family. I'm on my last load of the day. Let's all go feed my girls, then we will meet over at my house and make plans. Lone, you mean your wife's name is Little Bird?"

"Yes, W. P., my Little Bird and I have been married less than two years, and we are out traveling around and trying to find our roots."

"You don't know our Granny Little Bird. She is my grandmother and lives with us."

"It's going to take us a lifetime to tell each other our history."

W. P. squinted his beady family eyes at me and said, "Okay."

Little Bird and I loaded into his Chevy dully and traveled the grasslands of eastern Creek County. We found Slick, Bristow, Tuskegee, and the Deep Fork of the Canadian River, saw countless cow-calf pairs, and wouldn't you know it, they all came running toward the dully bawling their heads off. Little Bird and I had a treat that morning; it was like we were in a cage and all the cows were looking in at us. W. P. spread out a ton of range cubes and stated that he was through for the day. We traveled back to Depew, picked up our motor home and yellow Hummer, and followed W. P. to his ranch home just outside of town.

"Lone, park your motor home beside the garage for a plug-in, and I will go in and check to see if everybody is up and presentable. I need to tell you and your wife—

my wife died last year, and my mother and grandmother are living here with my six kids. We live like this to keep the family together; we all have health problems and wind up helping each other."

W. P. disappeared into his house, and almost immediately, the whole tribe was outside wanting to get in our motor home. Little Bird and I just stepped out and let them see to their hearts' content. Of all the hugging and kissing relations you have ever seen, we had it. We found six kids, Granny Little Bird, and W. P.'s mother, Sun Ray, to be such a delight. Dinner was a jump back in time—fry bread with bacon-flavored beans, and let me tell you, this Lone ate way too much.

Granny Little Bird took over the family history and told what she knew about the Feather clan moving into Creek County. My Little Bird and I got out all our papers and told our side of Miner Feather moving into Payne County. We compared notes, documents, land patents, signatures, pictures, physical evidence taken from Yonder Rock, and brought everybody into modern times. All W. P. could do was quietly sob, nod his head, and we all had a group hug that afternoon. We tied up all the loose strings, shared all the pictures, agreed on the family history, and decided to go out for supper. Our journey into Tulsa blew the sad feelings away, and Pizza Inn fed us all we could eat.

"Lone, I want you and Little Bird to go with me in the morning to feed. I have something to show you."

"Yes, we have something to show you too."

Little Bird and I laid out our cowboy garb that night and were ready for an early morning drive. The early morning "let's go" call came before daylight, just like I suspected. We traveled out in the grassland before the sun came up and found the old family graves on a small hill. W. P. led us to his wife's grave. There were several generations of headstones, including one marked Woodrow P. Olson, who died in 1840. The realization of history being revealed to me was a wake-up call; it was our time to sob. I snapped photos of all the headstones for the years to come. W. P. led us back to his dully, and we spent the rest of the morning feeding his girls, as he called them. Breakfast was a greasy spoon restaurant with eight stools in Slick, Oklahoma. It was one of the best country breakfasts in the county, according to W. P. Our travels back to Depew took us through the grasslands, where countless cows and calves were beside W. P.'s bull pasture. As he said before, he liked the Oklahoma black baldies. Every one of his bulls were long-body Angus of fine breeding.

"Lone, I need to ask you a question, and if you don't want to answer, that's alright with me. Granny Little Bird and I have an idea where the money came from for all this land that we have seen this morning. We own most of the land for miles in each direction and run these cows. Our forefathers came here from Georgia, split up, and as far as I know, Miner Feather was the only one that knew where the clans were. For some reason, we think that Miner found the gold across the Cimarron that belonged to the Cherokees and bought all this land from the Creek Nation under the name of my great-great-great-grandfather Woodrow P. Olson. We have the original land patent signed by Grandfather and witnessed by Miner Feather. Lone, you and I know the professors at the universities of the time wouldn't have sixty-four hundred dollars for twenty sections of land. We know that Miner was just that, a miner, and could dig faster than any two men and take a break in between. What do you think?"

"I have the answer for you. Let's have a family meeting, and I will lay it out for you." We arrived back in time for lunch and soon had all the kids ready for an afternoon nap. Granny, Sun Ray, W. P., Little Bird, and I had a comfortable seat at the kitchen table, where I started by asking if they had any lead marbles that looked like mine.

Granny was always one with a quick answer. "Yes, we know all about those lead marbles. They are worthless at today's lead prices. I don't know why I kept them; they are all in a tin under my bed."

"W. P., best we get the marbles out. I want to show you something. Sun Ray, would you close the drapes and turn out the lights?" W. P. brought the lead marbles, and I turned on the black light, and we had the most beautiful purple glow emit from the tin you could imagine. Even our hands had the telltale specks. "Okay, Sun Ray, you can turn on the lights now."

I started in Walnut Grove, Georgia, and told the complete story of Miner and his lead marbles—how he had helped the starving hoards of trail spent Indians, provided corn and beans to any tribe that was in need, tried to give away his complete cache of gold-covered lead marbles, and lived to be 104 years old. I then took a knife and cut the lead away from the gold and showed the Olson clan what they had all this time.

Granny was first. "You don't think that Miner found the gold of the Cherokees?"

"No, Granny Little Bird, that gold is still out there somewhere."

W. P. was next. "How much gold did Miner bring from Georgia?"

"According to Doctor Askin, who did the archeological analysis of Yonder Rock and its contents, there were almost thirty-eight million dollars in gold bullion moved in a double bottom Conestoga wagon. To answer your next question before you ask it, at today's prices of a thousand dollars per troy ounce, each one of those marbles are worth more than five thousand dollars per marble."

Granny grabbed the tin and counted out twenty-two of the marbles and came up with $110,000. All we could hear was a quick draw of air, then silence.

"Now folks, one last warning from me. The lead on the outside of the gold is very poisonous in the vapor form. Please don't try your hand at melting all this down. I have already lost a brother to this malady and would hate it if you were sickened with lead poisoning. The black light I used to show the purple dye is harmless but does show up very nicely."

"Who can melt all this lead off of the gold?" asked W. P.

"The archeologist showed me how to melt the gold in a kiln. Or a good goldsmith can, but be careful who you trust."

Granny, the outspoken one, came up with the next answer. "These marbles have come to me through the ages by my ancestors. I can see that you and your wife are trying to do what is right by telling all of us what we inherited. Don't you have a good church or mission you could donate all this to?"

"W. P., we sure don't need another source of income," Sun Ray said.

"Lone Feather, we give you these marbles to give to a needy church somewhere, and as you said, be careful when you melt the lead."

"Okay, Olson clan, we will melt the lead off and give the gold to the Cimarron Mission up by Pawnee. I don't think that all this information needs to be tattled to the four winds. It's best to let the Miner legacy live on to the glory of the Lord."

Little Bird and I traveled on the next day and realized there was no end to the intentions of Miner Feather. How long we would find those lead-covered marbles, we didn't know, but from the looks of Little Bird, I'd best get back to the old home place and build a large house with a baby crib close at hand.

Before we end the saga of Miner's Legacy, I moved the eleven hundred pounds of lead-gold ingots from the Arms room at Fort Sill to a foundry that specialized in gold smelting. We sold the gold at its highest price ever and started finding churches that were in building programs. Where the money came from to pay their debts, they never knew, and we never told.

e|LIVE

---

listen|imagine|view|experience

AUDIO BOOK DOWNLOAD INCLUDED WITH THIS BOOK!

In your hands you hold a complete digital entertainment package. Besides purchasing the paper version of this book, this book includes a free download of the audio version of this book. Simply use the code listed below when visiting our website. Once downloaded to your computer, you can listen to the book through your computer's speakers, burn it to an audio CD or save the file to your portable music device (such as Apple's popular iPod) and listen on the go!

How to get your free audio book digital download:

1. Visit www.tatepublishing.com and click on the e|LIVE logo on the home page.
2. Enter the following coupon code:
   d629-e042-a8d8-d0a4-28cb-acec-f3b2-7109
3. Download the audio book from your e|LIVE digital locker and begin enjoying your new digital entertainment package today!